Was it a calling card...or a warning?

"This arrow is exactly like the one you found yesterday," Luke told her.

A painful breath filled her lungs. The Hunter was back. While she'd been showing the sponsors around the island, the same man who'd held a knife to her throat twenty-four hours ago had shot an arrow into the wreckage of the obstacle course that nearly drowned them.

"So he's still here on the island, and he's toying with us." For a moment she felt so helpless that hot tears rushed to her eyes. Luke spread his arms wide and she stepped between them, looking for their comforting strength.

"So, the Hunter came back after stealing our boat yesterday?" she asked.

"Or he might be one of the four people back at the campsite right now," Luke said.

Something rustled in the forest behind them. They both spun sharply. She searched the tree line. She heard nothing but the whispers of trees in the breeze. The Hunter could be anywhere. Silent. Deadly. Now she knew: nowhere was safe.

Maggie K. Black is an award-winning journalist and romantic suspense author with an insatiable love of traveling the world. She has lived in the American South, Europe and the Middle East. She now makes her home in Canada with her history teacher husband, their two beautiful girls and a small but mighty dog. Maggie enjoys connecting with her readers at maggiekblack.com.

Books by Maggie K. Black

Love Inspired Suspense

Killer Assignment
Deadline
Silent Hunter

Visit the Author Profile page at Harlequin.com.

SILENT HUNTER

MAGGIE K. BLACK

HARLEQUIN® LOVE INSPIRED® SUSPENSE

Recycling programs
for this product may
not exist in your area.

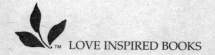 LOVE INSPIRED BOOKS

ISBN-13: 978-0-373-44652-0

Silent Hunter

www.Harlequin.com

Printed in U.S.A.

This is what the Sovereign Lord says to these bones:
I will make breath enter you, and you will come to life.
—Ezekiel 37:5

With thanks to all the amazing friends and camp staff
who helped me brainstorm for this book.
I couldn't have done it without you.

ONE

Worn wooden rungs creaked loudly under Nicky Trailer's boots. The ladder quivered as she climbed. She was a good twenty feet up in the air, smack-dab in the middle of Camp Spirit's main lodge, halfway between the old wooden floors and steeply slanted ceiling. The camp director's hazel eyes glanced up at the ceiling hatch high above her head. When she'd decided to store years' worth of paperwork up inside the claustrophobic crawlspace, she hadn't expected the camp's owner would ever send her on such a short-notice scavenger hunt. Especially not because he'd invited a reporter to the camp without telling her. "This still feels like a terrible idea."

"Oh, don't you worry, the loft's only three stories up, and here I seem to remember a certain tomboy in pigtails once being the youngest girl in camp history to conquer the high ropes." George Dale's warm chuckle echoed up the A-framed walls.

"That's not what I—" The words froze on her tongue as she caught the twinkle in the old man's eyes. Her elderly boss was teasing. As always. Apparently he wasn't the slightest bit worried about having some journalist poking around the day before she led the most important canoe trip of her life. *So why was she?*

"I was the youngest camper period, and don't you forget it." Nikki flashed a grin and tucked an unruly curl of long brown hair firmly back under her bandanna. "You're not getting out of discussing this reporter thing *that* easily. Though if I'd realized the loft ladder had gotten this creaky, I'd have added a new one of those to my wish list, too."

Right behind patching the roof, better sports equipment and rebuilding the boathouse. There were two months until summer camp and the list of things needing repair was growing longer by the day. Her gaze ran through towering glass windows, past the cabins, down to where the morning sun set rays of light dancing on the lake. She'd spent almost twenty years among these Ontario trees—first as camper, then counselor and now as George's second in command. Nicky ran Camp Spirit's summer and off-season camps, while George managed the business side. It was a great partnership that felt more like family than owner and employee.

If only our days weren't numbered. It was only a question of whether money troubles or George's failing health sank Camp Spirit first. His tendency to take on the neediest campers regardless of their ability to pay didn't leave much left over for new equipment and repairs. And while George's only son, Trevor, worked there occasionally, it was clear the young man would rather sell than fill his father's shoes.

Which is why tomorrow's trip is way too impor-

*tant to mess up by having some Toronto journalist tag
along.* George had invited a handful of community and
business leaders for a weekend of camping on an isolated Muskoka island. He'd pitched it as "three days
extreme camping, followed by a serious discussion
about investing in Camp Spirit's future." She wasn't
quite sure what kind of investment he had in mind,
but even a donation of volunteers or equipment could
mean staying open another summer or two. The trapdoor slid back easily. Dust and cobwebs filled the air.

"It's not that I don't trust you, but inviting any
media up at this point is just asking for bad press."
She climbed into the attic on her hands and knees. "Do
you want me to get a cabin ready for him?"

"Actually, he's staying with me." George looked up
at her through the hole in the floor. He ran one hand
along his white beard. "Mr. Wolf is coming up as a
friend, not a reporter. He's a really outstanding young
man, and I wanted to make sure you had a chance to get
to know him one-on-one, before everyone else arrived
tomorrow. I'm hoping you two will really hit it off."

What exactly did he mean by that? It would hardly
be the first time the widower had invited someone to
swing by in a misguided attempt at playing match-
maker. She pressed her lips together to keep from smiling. "Well, if he's a friend of yours, I'm sure we'll get
along as friends just fine."

She picked her way through mountains of old tarps
and sports equipment. George was an old softie, but
he had to know she had no intention of ever leaving
these woods, let alone following some man to the city.

Besides, it wasn't as though the camp didn't have a steady stream of healthy, God-fearing bachelors come tramping through.

Sure, the first time a cute guy held her hand by the water and said he liked her, she'd believed him with every beat of her foolish heart. She'd been eighteen then. Louie had been nineteen and a counselor from their rival camp, with sad gray-blue eyes and a white scar that curved at his throat. He'd left without even saying goodbye, and now after watching countless other camp romances flare up then fizzle out, it was clear that while the moonlight might bring out the romantic in people, they usually just ended up walking right back out of these woods as easily as they'd walked in.

A pile of old camp mats slithered apart underneath her. "Now, remind me what—"

The crash below was deafening. A wooden echo shook the floor beneath her. A cry rose to her lips but she bit it back. "George? What was that? Are you okay?"

Silence came from the hole in the floor. Her eyes glanced up toward the skylight for a second as she prayed. *Please, Lord, don't let it be another heart attack. He barely survived the last one.* She scrambled to the trapdoor and looked down. The ladder had fallen over. The dining hall was empty. Hopefully that meant he'd just gone to grab something. "Hey!" She kept her voice upbeat but loud. "Where'd you go? That ladder won't stand on its own."

Any response he might have given was lost in the

sound of a powerful engine peeling down the camp's gravel road. She slid over to the skylight and opened it. A black sports car pulled to a neat stop beside the lodge. A man stepped out. Nicky's mouth went dry. The visitor was tall, with tousled black hair and just the hint of three-o'clock shadow along his jaw. His broad shoulders were cleanly framed by the lines of a gray suit jacket. Sunglasses hid his eyes, while the crisp dress shirt did nothing to disguise the solid strength that lay beneath it. He loosened his tie just enough to undo his top button. A frown crossed his lips. Then he disappeared around the corner toward the office door.

This was Mr. Wolf? Nicky sat back on her heels and pressed her palm against her chest. Probably just as well her first glimpse of him was through the attic window. It would give her time to get the flush of heat out of her cheeks. She ran both hands down her dirty jeans and brushed the cobwebs from her face. Then she made her way through the maze of equipment back to the trapdoor.

"Hey, George? I think your reporter friend has pulled up outside. Also don't forget about the ladder."

A fit of coughing overtook her lungs. The air was thick and bitter. Thin fingers of smoke curled through the trapdoor, setting every warning bell inside her clanging. She braced her body and hung her head through the hole in the floor. Dark smoke poured from under the door leading to the kitchen. Orange flames flickered at the serving window. Panic flooded her veins, nearly sending her headfirst through the hole.

She was alone. She was trapped. And the building was on fire.

* * *

Searing heat shot through Luke's palm as his fingers brushed the doorknob. Gingerly he placed his hand flat against the office door. Warmth radiated through it. *Bad sign. Very bad sign.* The faintest whisper of smoke slipped from around the reinforced door and the lodge windows showed nothing but a reflection of trees. But somewhere inside the building a fire was raging.

He scanned the campgrounds. For a split second he thought he saw someone moving in the trees. A shadowy shape in what looked like hunting fatigues was pelting up a steep path through the woods.

"Hey! Stop! Someone needs help!" The figure disappeared and Luke grit his teeth. He didn't have time to chase after him. And, if his old and regrettable memories of teenage mischief were correct, it would take him at least twenty minutes to run to the neighboring camp. But only moments ago he'd seen a woman in the attic window. Had she managed to get out safely? *Being here is a painful reminder that I'm the last man any woman would want as a hero.*

Hero or not, he might be the only chance she had.

Stepping back from the door, he called up to the empty window. "Hey! I'm going to call the fire department and then I'm coming to get you out." There was no response but he couldn't afford to wait. Flames were now pouring through a broken window at the back of the building. Tongues of fire licked toward the sky as he pulled out his cell phone.

He couldn't get a signal, but he remembered seeing a red emergency telephone on a pole near the first-aid station. Luke ran for it, wrapped his jacket around his fist and smashed the glass. He wrenched the handset from the cradle. "Hello? Hello? Can anyone hear me?"

"Nine-one-one. Emergency services." The voice was crisp and female.

"I'm at Camp Spirit on rural route eight. The lodge is on fire and someone's inside."

"Emergency vehicles are being dispatched to your location, can you describe—"

"No. Sorry. I need to get her out of there."

He ran at the lodge and threw his weight into a solid blow aimed right at the center of the office door. It flew back off the hinges. Smoke poured out.

Sloshing his jacket in a rain barrel beside the door, he held it to his face and entered the building. A surge of hot air beat back against his body. He bowed his head and pushed through as smoke seared his lungs. It seemed as if the fire was fiercest in the back of the building, but it was only a matter of time before flames engulfed the office, too.

"Hello! Hey! Can anybody hear me?" A voice groaned in the darkness. "Hang on!"

In seconds he reached George. The one man Luke owed his entire life to lay pinned to the floor underneath a bookcase. He was pale but—*Thank God*—still conscious.

"It's me, Luke. I'm going to get you out of here."

Shoving the bookcase aside, he grasped George under both arms and pulled him out from under it. The air was getting hotter. The smoke was growing thicker.

His mind's eye set firmly on the faint shaft of daylight cutting through the darkness, he stumbled toward it.

Clean air filled Luke's lungs as he hauled George through the doorway and up onto the grassy slope. He knelt beside him.

"I called 9-1-1. Help is on the way. But I saw a woman in the window. She still in there?"

George nodded. "Nicky."

"How do I get to her? Stairs?"

"No. Just…ladder." George's voice was so faint Luke had to strain to catch his words. He turned back to the fire as George grabbed his arm. "Please… Take…like…" A fit of coughing stole George's words from his lungs. Tears filled his smoke-stained eyes. *"Cash box…"*

The words hit Luke like a slap in the face. Was George asking him to run into the fire to find the camp cash box? *Or was he intentionally reminding Luke of the very worst thing he'd ever done?*

There wasn't time for this. Shoving the question from his mind, Luke ran back toward the lodge, ignoring the pain in his lungs and the heat on his limbs. Soot coated his skin. He snapped off what remained of his tie, swinging loose over a shirt now more tatters than clothing.

A woman's scream filled the air. He rounded the corner and saw her.

"Nicky" dangled from the skylight window, climbing hand-over-hand down the slanted roof tiles using something that looked like a knotted tarp. *Clever.* But she was still almost three stories off the ground, with a sheer slide to the cement below. *The makeshift rope barely reached halfway to the ground.* He'd have to convince her to jump and find some way to break her fall. If he missed, she'd break every bone in her body.

Smoke poured through the window above her as he ran to her aid. He could hear sirens wailing in the distance.

The tarp chain snapped. Nicky flew backward through the air. Prayers for mercy poured wordlessly through his lips as he reached out. Her body hit his chest. The force knocked him back, throwing them to the ground. His arms tightened around her, absorbing the blow, as cement knocked the air from his lungs.

She lay on top of him for a moment, her back pressed against his chest. Her face turned towards him. Her breath came fast and hard on his neck. Wild, dark hair brushed against his face, filling his senses with haunting scents of wood smoke and wild berries. "It's okay. You're okay. I've got you."

"George… He…" She tried to speak, but could barely manage a whisper.

"He's all right. I got him out. You okay to walk? We'd better get away from this building."

She rolled off onto the ground beside him. He helped her to her feet, but they'd barely gone a few steps when he felt her fall against his shoulder.

"I'm sorry," she said. "I'm not hurt. Just shaky."

He wrapped his arm around her. "Take it slow. We'll get the paramedics to check you out."

Emergency vehicles poured down the camp driveway. Doors slammed. Voices shouted. Fire hoses roared to life.

"I'm Nicky Trailer, the camp director. Thank you for saving me."

"Luke Wolf, *Torchlight News*. You're very welcome." A smile turned at the corner of his lips. Then it froze as he looked down at her face. Luminous hazel eyes looked up into his, shining like gold in her soot-stained face and sending disjointed memories cascading through his mind. His heart stuttered.

That Nicky? Still here? This many years later? Could it really be her? If so, did she even have any idea who he was?

She stumbled. Her hand brushed against his, sending an unsettling shiver through his skin. Her gaze dropped to his where his shirt laid torn open over his chest. A gasp slipped through her lips. Her eyes grew wider as she pushed him away and stumbled backward.

"Louie? Is it really you?" She crumpled to the ground.

TWO

The afternoon sun had already begun its trek toward the top of the tree line when a police officer dropped Nicky back at the camp to grab a few things from her cabin and pick up her car. They didn't want her spending the night at the main site until the investigation into the fire was complete. Not even in her own cabin, her own bed. At least the police had no problem with her still taking George's potential donors on the camping trip tomorrow, given they'd be canoeing to a small island and not staying at the main site. A trip she'd now make with only Trevor for part-time backup, since George would be in hospital.

The lodge's burned-out shell rose in front of her, wrapped in a maze of yellow police tape. Her chest ached as if someone had reached into her center and hollowed it out. Her mind spun with the list of jobs she needed to get done before she left to spend the night on a friend's couch. But before she did anything, she should probably take a few minutes to settle her heart. She turned right and wound her way through the thick woods to the south of the camps. Then she started climbing.

Her legs felt like sandbags. The sprinkler system and fire alarm had both failed. A brief conversation with someone from the insurance company told her they'd be investigating two possibilities: major electrical fault and arson. Which was worse? The idea the camp was in such bad repair that it had become a dangerous firetrap? Or that someone had intentionally tried to destroy the camp, her home? Both were unthinkable.

She took a deep breath and pushed her body through the branches. The toes of her boots dug hard into the steep, narrow trail. Her mind pushed prayers to the tip of her tongue. Thanking God that George was alive and resting in hospital. Thanking God that the fire hadn't spread to the forest. Thanking God that Luke Wolf had been there...

As Luke's name crossed her lips, suddenly the blue-gray eyes of the teenaged boy who'd once stolen her heart among these trees filled her mind. She grabbed a narrow trunk with one hand to steady herself as she suddenly remembered what she'd done—

Just before she'd passed out, she'd asked the man who'd caught her if he was the same guy she'd known as "Louie."

What had she been thinking? It had been years since she'd stopped wishing that boy would ever return and apologize. Let alone feeling a flutter of hope every time she knew a man named Louie, Louis or Lou was about to come through the door. The nineteen-year-old rival camp counselor had broken her heart more than ten years ago. Guys like that didn't just come back after a decade, all grown up in a sharp suit and tie, just to pluck her from danger.

Yet, for a moment, she'd thought she'd seen the same white, telltale scar curving along the lines of his soot-stained chest. Maybe it had just been her mind playing tricks. Everything that had happened between seeing those flames and waking up in the back of an ambulance was still all a blur.

Thick forest gave way to the edge of a sheer rock cliff. It was the highest point of the property. Nothing but sharp rock lay below, on all sides of the lookout. Yet if she raised her chin toward the horizon, sparkling blue waters filled her eyes. Dark clouds gathered in the distance.

Once this had just been the place she'd come as a teenager to meet her secret crush from the camp next door. Now, as a woman, it was the old familiar ground she'd been walking daily, for years, to pray in solitude. Below her to the right lay the glistening buildings and sparkling beach of Ace Sports Resort. To her left, she caught a glimpse of the burned remains of Camp Spirit's lodge. She dropped to her knees and let her forehead fall into her hands.

Oh, Lord, I don't even know what to pray right now.

Footsteps crackled in the brush behind her. She jumped up. It was Luke. The sport's reporter had changed into jeans and a plaid shirt, but somehow still managed to look as though he'd just stepped out of a magazine. Clouds reflected in the sunglasses hiding his eyes. Faint soot still traced the deepest lines of his face, as if someone had just sketched him out of charcoal.

It had to be him! How else would he have known where to find her?

"Hey!" Luke started toward her. "How are you feeling? You okay?"

She nodded. "Yeah. I'm fine."

He reached out as though unsure whether to shake her hand or to hug her. Then he stopped and shoved his hand into his pocket. "How's George?"

"He's okay. The doctors only let me talk to him for a few minutes. But he seems good. They're just worried about his heart and want him to rest in the hospital for a couple of days. Canoe trip is still going ahead tomorrow, though. His son, Trevor, is going to alternate between camping with us and being back here for his dad."

"Glad to hear it. I filed a police report. I think I might have seen someone in the woods just before I called 9-1-1."

She rolled her shoulders back, like a duck shaking off water. "Thanks. But, honestly, I'm not ready to believe anyone would have set this fire intentionally."

Luke paused, then ran his hand over his jaw. His index finger brushed over his bottom lip as if trying to summon words he wasn't sure how to say.

"We need to talk."

She pressed her lips together and took a deep breath.

"Told you we'd find her here!" a voice boomed.

Neil Pryce, the director of Ace Sports Resort, came crashing through the underbrush. The former quarterback jammed a very large smartphone into his jacket pocket. "Sorry to leave you back there, Luke, but I had a quick email to sort and I knew that I'd probably lose our Wi-Fi signal once I left Ace Sports territory."

So much for their moment alone to talk.

Neil reached for Nicky's hand and squeezed like clamped-on jumper cables. "I'm so sorry to hear about what happened. A fire. Wow. Well, I guess that's the danger you run with those rustic older buildings."

She smiled politely and pulled her hand away. "I didn't realize you two knew each other. Though unless I have him mistaken for someone else, I think Luke used to be a counselor at Ace Sports? Back when we were both teenagers?"

Neil's grin grew so wide and toothy it reminded her of a shark. "Really? I didn't know Ace Sports actually had an alumni working as a Toronto sports reporter."

Luke pulled off his sunglasses. Gray eyes searched her face. "Sorry, I never actually went to Ace Sports or worked there. I've never been a camp counselor kind of guy. In fact, my first legit job was actually stacking newspapers in the warehouse at *Torchlight News*. George helped me get it."

Nicky felt her heart drop a couple of inches. Did that mean he wasn't who she thought he was?

"Well, it's never too late to get the Ace Sports experience," Neil said. "Me and Luke met at the hospital. I could hear the sirens all the way from the tennis courts, so figured I'd follow the ambulance to the hospital to see if there was anything I could do to help."

She nearly snorted. It was more likely Neil had

hoped to take advantage of George's enfeebled state to snag a few of their potential donors for his latest vanity project. Neil might be the boss of the shiny camp next door, but he wasn't an owner. He simply reported to a whole boardroom full of money-minded shareholders who'd probably love to snatch up Camp Spirit's land to build another luxury sports complex. If the lodge fire did turn out to be arson, would police be questioning Neil and his staff? Neil might be both competitive and smarmy, but she hated to think he was actually capable of stooping that low.

"When I discovered Luke here was a sports reporter, I offered to put him up in one of Ace Sports' deluxe chalets," Neil added. "Just finished moving him in. In return, we're hoping he'll give us some positive press on our new facilities. An hour in our heated pool and he won't be able to help himself from giving us a full spread."

No surprise there. Nicky's smile stiffened. Here George had assured her that Luke was a good friend, not the kind of person who would run to their competitor in exchange for a comfier bed and hot towels. Now she just had to hope she could keep the prospective donors from deserting them, as well.

Luke felt something twist in his chest as he saw the disappointment flicker in Nicky's dark eyes. Not that the rest of her face gave that much away.

"Well, then, I guess Camp Spirit's loss is Ace Sports' gain." She flashed him a crisp, professional smile, which somehow managed to make him feel even worse. What else had she expected him to do? George was in the hospital. The closest hotel was an hour away.

Luke ran his hand across the back of his neck. "Actually, *Torchlight News* has a policy of never exchanging publicity for perks. The paper will pay for my stay."

"Well, I'm sure you'll find it quite comfortable." Nicky's smile never faltered. "Now, if you'll excuse me, I'm taking a group canoeing this weekend and need to take a boat to the campsite to make sure everything is in order." Before he could say anything more, she turned on her heel and disappeared into the woods.

Neil chuckled. "She's a pip, isn't she? I pity the poor fool who ever tries to tame her. Now, how about you and I go take a tour of Ace Sports' new facilities? Maybe try out the pool? Or are you more of an archery man?"

Luke blew out a hard breath. Shooting off a few arrows sounded like exactly what he could use right now. In fact, he had his wooden bow stashed in the back of his car, just in case he was able to get some target practice in at the archery range. But, between the admission that he'd never actually been an Ace Sports counselor and where he was crashing overnight, he'd somehow just managed to make Nicky even more upset than she was already. He had to fix this.

"Maybe later." He glanced down the hill, searching for some sign of her among the trees. "Thank you again for your help. I'll find my own way back in a bit and check in with your front office later."

Luke started down the hill, half jogging and half climbing. She'd been in such a hurry she'd just run off straight through the trees instead of bothering with the winding path. Same old Nicky. Sure, the past decade had softened some of the angles. But that fire in her eyes hadn't dampened for a moment.

He lost sight of her at the beach, behind a rack of canoes, but saw her again by the docks. She disappeared into the boathouse. He followed, took a deep breath and slid the door open. The boathouse was built like a barn with thin docks forming two separate channels. Faint light filtered through the windows, bouncing off the water and sending refracted light across the walls. Two identical four-person speedboats sat side by side. The door swung shut behind him. "Hello? Nicky?"

A figure rose from the back of the nearest boat. A dark raincoat now engulfed her body. The hood framed her face, casting shadows down the curve of her neck. Dark curls trailed along her cheeks. His heart caught in his chest. All these years, Nicky had been like a phantom at the edges of his memory—and here she was even more beautiful than he'd remembered.

How much did she remember? Did she remember the long conversations on top of the cliff? How he'd opened his heart to her? How close they'd gotten? Or had everything they'd shared been destroyed by how he'd left, then been lost under an avalanche of time?

Her eyes opened wide. Then they narrowed, filling with a look that bordered on frustration. He took a deep breath and reminded himself that he'd walked out of her life for a reason. He'd needed to protect her then. He needed to protect her now. "Sorry to just barge in like this. We didn't really didn't get a chance to talk back there, and I wanted to make sure everything was okay."

"Yeah, I'm just busy doing the work of two people, trying to get ready for tomorrow." She shrugged. "Obviously, I'll feel better when George is back on his feet again. I'm guessing you didn't get a chance to talk to him?"

A bitter taste rose to his tongue. Yeah, he'd talked to George, for all of two seconds after he'd pulled him from the blaze. Just long enough for George to remind him he'd once been a liar and a thief who'd tried to steal the camp cash box. Which was the exact opposite of what he'd have ever expected from the old man, especially after George had pressed upon him how important it was to him personally that Luke come up this weekend. It made no sense.

"Not really. Just a few words. Do you keep anything special in your camp cash box? I thought he said something about my going back for it, but obviously I couldn't."

She blinked. "No. Just a couple hundred dollars in petty cash. Nothing worth running into a fire for. Maybe you misunderstood him."

He shrugged. "Probably." She turned to the boat. He crossed the floor in three steps. "Wait. Before you go, I owe you an apology."

She didn't even look at him. "Don't worry about it. Please. You're hardly the first person Ace Sports has lured away. Just make sure you double check your invoice carefully." She slapped a button on the wall and the garage-type door rolled open. "Now, if you could close this door after I leave, I'd really appreciate it. The remote isn't working and it's going to rain."

Why were they still talking to each other like virtual strangers? For years he'd pictured what it would be like to see Nicky again. He'd imagined her crying. He'd imagined her yelling. He'd even imagined her tumbling into his arms. He'd never imagined her just brushing him off.

She glanced back over her shoulder. Her eyes met his. Huge. Fathomless. Filled with questions she didn't seem ready put into words, yet which still somehow managed to reach into his chest begging him for the answers. She slipped a key into the ignition. The engine roared to life.

"Nicky, wait." He crossed the floor quickly, feeling all the words he wanted to say get mixed up and jumbled inside him. Thunder rumbled in the distance.

"I'm sorry, but I really must go." The boat inched forward. She didn't even look at him. "I've got to get the camping site ready for tomorrow and the storm's moving faster than I expected. I'm short-handed as it is—"

He grabbed the corner of the windshield. "I'm sorry I never showed up at the lookout that day and just left you standing there waiting. I never should've left without saying goodbye. As for telling you my name was 'Louie' instead of 'Luke' so you couldn't find me, and pretending I was really a counselor at Ace Sports... that was pretty low."

A long pause spread through the tiny boathouse, filling his ears with the sound of water lapping against the boat. Her hood fell back. Her eyes were wet with unshed tears. Her lower lip trembled. He slid his hand down the windshield and onto the console, inches away from hers.

But she kept both hands on the steering wheel. When she spoke, her voice was as clear and strong as the sound of the final whistle. "I don't know what to say to that. Except, thank you for finally being honest. I thought I'd recognized you earlier, but I didn't know what to think, especially when you said you'd never worked at Ace Sports." She blinked hard. "I accept your apology. But I honestly don't have time to talk about this right now. I just really have to go."

"Okay." He let go of the boat and crossed his arms. "Then I'm coming with you."

THREE

The thick mass of towering rock and dense pines rose out of the water, deep in the middle of the lake. Black-and-orange clouds hung heavy in the trees. Nicky eased up on the throttle and steered the boat toward the island. They'd barely exchanged more than a word or two since they'd left camp. Not that it was always easy to make yourself heard over the rush of the wind and the smack of waves hitting the boat. Maybe he was simply waiting for her to say something, but she didn't have a clue what to say.

So, her first love hadn't just broken her heart, he'd lied to her about who he was and where he was from. Repeatedly and intentionally. Which probably meant he'd just been some bored teenager from a nearby cottage who'd thought it would be fun to sneak into a camp. Wouldn't be the only time that had happened. Except, this time she'd been the foolish girl who'd been too quick to trust and to give her heart away. A mistake she wouldn't make again.

Nicky focused on coasting the boat through an obstacle course of jutting rocks and yellow buoys. Whatever she'd once felt for this man was ancient history. All that mattered now was saving her camp. Luke was nothing more to her now than someone her boss had invited up for the weekend.

She cut the motor, filling the air with a silence that was so still it was almost deafening.

Luke whistled under his breath. "George told me that a former camper had given Camp Spirit an actual island in their will, but I've never seen it."

She almost smiled. "It's about a two-hour trip by canoe, though way less by motorboat. It was bequeathed to Camp Spirit about three years ago, but we haven't been able to do much with it, to be honest. George has this vision of turning it into an offshoot youth camp for older teens that are either in trouble with the law or at risk of going that way. But we don't have the resources to make it happen."

"Do you get a lot of donations?"

She steered the boat toward a small strip of beach. "Not really. A few former campers give us twenty or thirty dollars a month. But even though George kind of runs the place like a charity, he's never applied to legally become one because we don't hit all the criteria, and that turns off a lot of donors. Sometimes business people or organizations partner with us to build something specific. And then there's Mystery Donor."

His eyebrows rose. "'Mystery Donor'?"

"That's what the counselors call him or her. Seven or eight years ago, someone gave George a huge, huge donation. Close to a million dollars, actually. With careful management, George was able to use it to fund new buildings and new projects. It kept us going for years. But as only George knew their name, the summer staff got into the habit of praying, 'Thank You, God, for the Mystery Donor!' and it stuck."

She chuckled. But Luke frowned. His gaze ran over the steep stone crags. His brow furrowed. The whole trip there she'd been catching little sideways glimpses of him, without really meaning to. Evaluating the man he was against the boy she remembered. His shoulders had gone from husky to strong. Dark stubble on his jawline hinted of a man who didn't like a close shave. No ring on his finger, implying he'd never settled down. There was still a slight curve at the corner of a mouth that looked just as soft as the day he'd first kissed her. "Well, I know things are tight financially, and I wish I had the kind of money that could help you guys out."

"Oh, trust me, you're not the only one. Just because I love working for George, doesn't mean I'm ever going to have the amount of money to buy this place out from under him. The land itself is worth far, far more than the business standing on it." She reached to touch his shoulder. Then caught herself midair. "You're a sport's reporter, not a millionaire."

"George asked me to come up because he had something important to talk to me about before the canoe trip. Do you know what it was?"

She sat straight. "No. I honestly don't." For that matter she didn't really know why George had wanted her to take down the old boxes of camp records and photographs. "I just presumed he wanted to talk to you about a newspaper article."

To their left, an aquatic obstacle course hung over the surface of the water in a collection of nets, tires and climbing ropes. They glided past it. Then, to the right, they could see the small sliver of murky sand that formed the island's only beach. A thin wooden dock ran along one side of it with a red-and-white sign that warned potential trespassers they were entering Camp Spirit property. She tossed the rope around a pillar, caught it on the first try and pulled the craft in to the dock.

They climbed out and she sighed. The beach was a mess of driftwood and seaweed. Trevor was supposed to have done a proper cleanup of the campsite earlier in the week. Apparently he hadn't bothered.

"Looks like I'm going to need two pairs of hands, after all. I'll run ahead to the campsite and make sure it's not a mess. If you could stay here and clear some of this mess off the beach…that would be amazing."

"You sure you're okay going off alone, after everything that happened this morning?" Luke sounded concerned. He had no reason to be. Whether they were on the mainland or the island, this camp was still her baby.

"Absolutely. You're probably more sore from catching me that I am from crashing into you." Light rain began to fall, dimpling the water and denting the mud by her feet. She started up the beach. The ground was scuffed with footprints. Even worse. Trespassers always made a mess of things. "Also, it looks like the island had a visitor recently. Fortunately, whoever they were, they're gone now, otherwise their boat would still be here. There's nowhere else on the island they could've safely moored."

Luke ran his hand through his hair. "Thanks again for letting me come with you. I know this isn't the ideal place for us to talk, but I thought it was important we cleared the air as soon as possible." There was a smile back in his voice again.

But this time she didn't smile back. Between the rain, Trevor's failure to get his work done and the signs of a trespasser, her evening had just gotten a whole lot busier. "I appreciate that. But it's okay. Really. You've apologized. I've accepted it. And I had a whole half-hour-long boat ride to let it sink in." *Because that's what adults did in situations like this. They got over things. They didn't let themselves fall into a cute guy's arms and cry, no matter how stressed, worried and tired they felt.*

She turned toward the woods. Branches were broken along the path that led to the campsite. Whoever had stopped by the island had also done some exploring while they were here. There was an arrow imbedded in the tree ahead of her. Slim, vicious, with jagged metal in the head. A titanium hunter's arrow. She grit her teeth and yanked it out of the wood. "Looks like our trespasser is also a hunter, and decided to use the trees for target practice."

Luke snorted. "Well, that's a super-expensive arrow for someone to go shooting into trees on a little island like this. That's the kind of gear you'd expect from someone who'd just dropped a few thousand bucks on a high-tech compound bow because they figured they'd go illegally bag a few bears or moose."

She blinked. He was absolutely right. But she hardly expected Luke to know that. "You know archery?"

"Now I do." He stepped closer and looked down at the arrow in her hands. "Been taking lessons for years and brought my bow up just in case I got the chance to shoot a few at your range on the mainland. I didn't actually know the first thing about archery back when you knew me before. Just pretended I did to impress you. But the way you used to talk about it left me itching to try it. Even learned enough woodworking to make my very own recurve bow."

Her heart stopped. She'd been huge into woodwork that summer, too, and had spent days carving him something special. She could still remember the pounding in her chest when she'd handed him the wooden animal she'd carved. Not to mention her devastation when she'd run to their meeting spot the next day to find it empty and wondered if her clumsy attempt at a gift had been what scared him off. Despite everything her brain might say, her heart could remember it like yesterday.

"Are you sure you're okay?" His chest was so close she could almost see his breath rise and fall. The raincoat he'd grabbed from the boat still hung open. The shirt underneath was almost soaked through. "Look, I know you said you're okay to just head off alone. But I can tell you're upset. I can see it in your eyes. I get you're just being professional about everything and I really respect that. But don't feel like you have to put on a brave face around me. We used to tell each other everything, Nicky. We used to be friends. If there's anything I can do, I want to help."

She bit her lip. The memory of his arms wrapped around her swept through her core like a visceral ache. Yeah, she wanted a hug. No, she wasn't about to let him give it. "No, Luke. *I* used to tell *you* everything. I was honest with you. That apparently never cut both ways." She sighed. "And it was probably a mistake to let you come along."

She tossed the arrow onto the beach and strode up the hill.

He watched her go, feeling his gut sink into the sand at his feet.

He'd hurt her. Badly.

Did she honestly believe everything they'd shared back then had been a lie? Yes, he'd only given her a nickname and he'd hidden where he was from—both rotten things to have done. But everything he'd felt for her and everything she'd meant to him had made it the most real and honest human connection he'd ever had in his life. Not that she was likely to ever believe that now.

His mind filled with memories of just a few hours earlier—her body crashing into his arms, relief filling his chest, the smell of her smoky hair as they fell backward onto the ground.

Thank You, God, that I actually did right by her, at least once in my life.

He grabbed a hunk of driftwood and threw it hard

into the bushes. It wasn't as though things would be any better if he told her the whole story. He'd been a petty thief and a runaway, sleeping in an abandoned cabin and scrounging whatever he could steal. The last time they'd met, he'd realized they'd grown too emotionally close and he hadn't wanted to risk getting caught. So he'd broken into George's office and tried to steal the camp's cash box. George had caught him and carted him off to the police to spend the night in a jail cell. Then, the next morning, the first man of God he'd ever met had come back, given him the cash box money for his bail, let him detox off drugs on his couch and helped him by offering him a chance to earn himself a life he could be proud of.

And I did everything in my power to pay him back for that, every chance I got.

The sound of Nicky running through the woods faded to silence. He had a pretty good guess about what would happen if he told her all that. Her walls would fall and her heart would overflow with compassion. She'd always been far more caring than a jerk like him had deserved.

He didn't deserve her sympathy. And she deserved better than him.

A scream split the air. Loud. Terrified.

"Nicky!" He ran toward the noise. Branches struck his body. His heart smacked hard in his chest. Her screams seemed to come from all directions at once. Then the wall of trees gave way to a clearing and a ring of tent platforms on cinder-block bases.

Nicky was down in the dirt, her face pressed into

the ground. A figure stood over her. The man's form was lost in hunting fatigues and a green balaclava. A compact hunter's compound bow hung on a strap across his back. With one hand the hunter clenched the back of her head. With the other he pressed the tip of a knife against her throat. She looked over at Luke. Tears poured down her cheeks.

Dear God, please don't let him hurt her. Help me save her.

Thunder rumbled in the skies above them. Luke held Nicky's gaze, steady and solid. "It's going to be okay, Nicky. I promise." The determination to keep her safe pulsed through his veins. It had been a long time since Luke had found himself at the wrong end of a criminal's knife. But the instincts that he'd once learned as a teenaged runaway had never left him. Luke turned to face her captor. His hands rose in front of him. His palms were open. But his body was tensed for a fight, if it came to that. "Let her go and no one needs to be hurt."

Silence filled the clearing—punctuated only by the sound of Nicky's ragged breath and the light patter of rain. The hunter's grip loosened just enough that she could crawl on her hands and knees, then he yanked Nicky's head back. She winced, but didn't give him the satisfaction of whimpering. Her eyes hadn't left Luke's face for a moment.

Luke stepped forward. "This is your last warning." His fingers tightened into fists. "You so much as bruise her skin and I will take you down."

Lightning flashed and then the skies opened. Heavy

rain pelted the ground. The man tossed his head back and laughed. Nicky kicked back hard. Her heel caught her captor hard in the gut. Luke charged. He caught the masked man by the throat and tossed him to the ground. Within seconds the hunter had sprung back to his feet. The knife blade flashed in his hand. But before Luke could even raise his hand to land a blow, the man took off running through the woods.

For half a second Luke watched him go, fighting the urge to chase him down. Instead, he dropped to his knees beside Nicky. "Are you okay? Did he hurt you?"

"I'm okay." She raised her face toward him. Her hair fell tangled and wild over her face. Rain and tears ran mingled down her cheeks. "I don't even know what happened. I walked into the campsite and he just jumped me from behind."

He helped her to her feet. Nicky's fingers ran down her muddy limbs as if she was taking inventory. "I didn't even think he wanted to hurt me at first. It was more like he wanted to scare me. But when he laughed at you like that—"

The roar of an engine filled the air.

"No!" Nicky took off running through the trees. Luke pelted after her. The forest gave way to a slab of granite rock. In the water below, a small boat was speeding away from the island. She sank to her knees. "He just stole our boat."

FOUR

"The keys were in the ignition." The words slipped through her lips and into the pouring rain as little more than a sigh of frustration. It had never even crossed her mind the trespasser might still be on the island. Let alone that he'd attack her and steal their boat.

"It's going to be okay." Luke squeezed her shoulder. His fingertips touched just below her shoulder blade. It was the kind of simple gesture that would seem natural coming from a close friend or colleague. But as Luke's fingers brushed her aching muscles she could feel her body relax. There'd always been something about the simplest touch of his hand that had made her feel safe. Back when she'd been young enough to think she needed a guy in her corner and foolish enough to believe it would be him.

Another flash of lightning forked through the sky, followed by the rumble of thunder.

"Of course we're going to be fine." She gripped the hood of her raincoat with both hands and pulled it up briskly. "The Hunter obviously got here in some kind of boat. Canoe probably. Maybe a kayak. All we have to do is find it and use it to get back to the mainland. The first priority, though, is getting off this rock. We don't want to get caught out either on the lake or in the trees while there's a risk of lightning. Fortunately this island has caves."

They picked their way back through the empty campground and then hiked through the forest into the center of the island. Finally they reached a place where a gaping hole cut deep into the side of the rock. They stepped into the mouth of the cave and out of the rain.

Luke glanced into the darkness. "How deep does it go?"

"Pretty deep. But it also gets really steep and narrow. We boarded it up a few yards in to stop anyone from going too far. Rumor is, though, if you go deep enough you'll eventually come out somewhere on the coast."

"You've never tried?"

"Never wanted to. It's pitch-black down there and turns into almost a sheer drop." She shivered. Sometimes they'd take campers right up to the barrier and turn off their flashlights, just so they could experience how dark the world could be.

Luke leaned back against the damp, stone wall. "I'm sorry. I didn't even think for a moment that whoever I saw running into the trees back on the mainland would ever come to the island and threaten you."

Her eyebrows rose. "Why would you?"

"Because I saw a man in hunting fatigues outside the lodge when it was on fire, and then one attacks you here now. You don't see an obvious connection there?"

She sighed. Just because she used to buy his stories, didn't mean she was just going to agree with whatever theories he came up with now. "A lot of people wear hunting fatigues up here. It's like someone from the city seeing two people in suits in the same day."

"But you can't discount the possibility someone is actually trying to hurt you or Camp Spirit. Look, if the person running through the trees is linked to this, he might have been heading to Ace Sports Resort—"

"Or to the highway. Or to someone's cottage. Or it could've just been another trespasser. We do get a lot of them." *Including apparently you.*

Nicky slid down the wall and sat on the floor. "Neil is very competitive and I don't like how he runs the place, but that doesn't make him a criminal. Also, I don't see how the lodge catching fire and a trespasser on the island could be connected. Two very different things happened in two completely different places."

"On the same day." Luke sat opposite her. "I just think it's too convenient to be a coincidence, don't you?"

"You sound like a reporter." She reached behind her neck and parted her hair down the middle. Then she twisted each half around her fingers to wring out the water. A deep, soft chuckle coaxed her eyes back to his face. "What's so funny?"

Luke looked down. "Sorry. Just seeing you do that gave me a flash of déjà vu. I always remember you having these long, curly pigtails, and you were always fiddling with them. It was cute."

She paused, her fingers still in her hair. Did he remember how he used to take her pigtails in his hands and gently tug her toward him until her lips met his? She stuffed her hands into her pockets. Well, she wasn't that girl anymore. "Grab any dry leaves or twigs if you can. I'm going to build a fire and see about drying us out."

There were waterproof matches in her jacket. It didn't take too long before they had a fledgling fire burning. Flames crackled softly. A long pause spread between them punctuated by the sound of rain lashing the trees, thunder sounding in the distance and the drip of water running down the cave.

"You sure our best option is to look for the Hunter's boat?" Luke asked. "There's no chance someone will come looking for us?"

"No." She sighed. "I'm sorry. George would've. But the only other person on-site now is Trevor, and he probably won't realize there's something wrong until sometime tomorrow. Have you ever met him?"

"Trevor?" Luke turned his face toward the sheet of rain. "Years ago."

"Well, Trevor's just kicking around for a few weeks, trying to scrounge up enough to go traveling again. He's the kind of guy who hates the idea of being tied down to anything." She frowned. "I can't imagine him keeping the place after George is gone."

Luke nodded slowly. "Is it possible that he had something to do with all this?"

"Trevor? No!" *First Neil, now Trevor? Was he still beating the bushes for random suspects?* "Look, Trevor knows he's going to inherit this whole place—

mainland and island—from George one day. As Trevor likes to keep reminding us, the camp may be struggling, but the land is worth a lot. He keeps pushing his dad to invest in things that push the property value up. Setting dangerous fires that could've destroyed the forest and allowing scary trespassers who could randomly attack strangers are exactly the kinds of thing that do the opposite of that. Now, if George and Trevor had any enemies who wanted to both see the camp fail and the land become unsellable, that would be different."

"Like someone at Ace Sports?"

They were back to suspecting Neil again? She rolled her eyes. This was the problem with random theories. Suddenly everyone was a suspect, whether it was logical or not.

Luke pulled his raincoat off and spread it on the ground. His shirt was so wet it almost looked as though someone had painted it across his chest. He rolled up his sleeves and undid the top buttons of his shirt.

She tried not to stare at how the firelight danced along his skin. Her eyes slowly traced the snakelike scar cutting into his skin. She jumped to her feet. "I don't believe it. You even lied to me about your scar."

"I did what?" His face was blank.

She leaned forward and pointed at the puckered white line that gashed across his perfect golden chest. "You told me that you'd been bitten by a dog, and I believed you, just like I believed every other lie. But I've seen enough camp injuries over the years to distinguish one kind of scar from another." Her fingers brushed the edge of his shirt. "That's a burn."

* * *

He winced as he watched the sting of betrayal fill her eyes. Well, of course he'd told her that. He'd been both too immature and frightened back then to even consider telling her the truth. Moments such as this made it hard to forgive himself for the man he used to be.

"Looks like you were just incapable of telling the truth about anything. How ironic you became a journalist."

He leaped to his feet. "Nicky, wait—"

"The lightning has stopped, and we've got a boat to find."

"Please. Let me explain." He reached for her hand.

She pulled away. "What could you possibly say now that would make any of this okay? I *cherished* my happy memories of you. Don't you get that? Even though you'd left. Even though you'd hurt me, I could still look back and know that just once in my life I had a short, perfect, summer romance with an incredible guy. Something *real* and true, that nothing else ever compared with since.

"I told the story of you to so many heartbroken teenagers who needed to know that they'd get over their first breakup, too. But now you've just turned up and trashed every good memory I had. You've erased any good feelings I was able to have looking back. Part of me almost wishes you'd just left me with my happy memories, whether they were true or not." She turned to the rain. "Yes, I do forgive you. I'll be professional about this weekend and I get that right now we're in this mess together. But as far as the past is concerned, I don't want to hear it."

"Fine. Then just look." He pulled his shirt open, feeling the buttons pop one by one. Then he slowly peeled his arm out of the sleeve. She gasped as her gaze traced the labyrinth of burn scars running down his chest and shoulders.

"What happened?" Her voice brushed softly through the dark air. The cave walls seemed to shrink around them.

"Boiling water. My mom said she spilled it by accident, but I don't really know. I was pretty little at the time, and my mom spent most of my childhood drunk. So it's hard to know what to believe."

Her fingers slid through his. "I'm sorry. How did your dad—?"

"Never met him. Which was a good thing." His voice sounded gruff. She was so close now he could almost feel her untamed hair brushing against his jaw. Had he pulled her toward him without realizing it? Or was she the one who'd drawn closer to him?

"Look, I'm genuinely sorry that I hurt you. I wish I could turn back time and undo every lie I ever told. When you met me I was nothing but a runaway teen with a criminal record for shoplifting and petty theft, hiding out in an abandoned cabin. Definitely not a camp counselor, let alone at Ace Sports." The back of his fingers touched her cheek. "You listened to me, Nicky. You prayed for me. You were the first decent, kind person I'd ever met in my life. I repaid you with lies, and I didn't have a clue how to love you. Not like how you loved me. But leaving you was the kindest thing I could've done, and I don't regret it."

She stepped back. A light flickered in the woods. Then a bright flashlight beam swung across her face, just long enough for Luke to see the deep pain echoing in her eyes.

"Hello? Nicky?" The voice was male, young and uncertain. "You out here?"

"Trevor? Yeah! Yeah, we're here!" She glanced back toward Luke. Then she ran out into the storm.

FIVE

The Friday morning sun beat down against the surface of the lake. Luke stood on the hill on the edge of Ace Sports' property. He watched as a lithe, dark-haired figure in jeans and a plaid shirt arranged canoes down the beach, their bows jutting out into the water. He sighed and pulled out his cellphone. Thankfully, he was still in range to use Ace Sports' Wi-Fi signal.

Nicky had barely said two words to him last night after Trevor had rescued them. To anyone else it would've probably looked as though she was just relieved George's son had taken the initiative to come looking for her and was in a hurry to file a police report about the stolen boat. Not to mention exhausted. But even through her relief, he'd seen just how tightly she'd pressed her lips together and how she hadn't once looked his way. Well, he was sorry if he'd destroyed her fantasy of what they'd once had, but the truth was leaving her then had been the right thing to do.

His phone began to ring. It was Jack Brooks, *Torchlight*'s most tenacious crime reporter and a solid friend.

"Hey! How goes the book tour? As glamorous as they say?"

"Sure." Jack laughed. "If your idea of glamor is drinking coffee in a highway hotel while your fiancée's half a country away planning your wedding. Got your voice mail. I thought you were in a forest this weekend?"

Cars were pulling into Camp Spirit's parking lot. Luke watched as Nicky left the beach and strode up to greet them. "I am. Arrived yesterday. That's what I wanted to talk to you about." Luke quickly filled his colleague in on both the fire and what had happened on the island.

Jack whistled. "So obviously you think there's a connection between the fire and this hunter guy?"

Relief spread over Luke's shoulders. *It felt good to hear someone else say it!* This is exactly why he knew he'd been right to call a fellow reporter. "Yeah, *I* do. But the police don't and Nicky doesn't. I don't even know for sure the man I saw running away from the lodge is the same man who jumped us on the island. Honestly, I was half expecting you to tell me I was crazy."

Jack's chuckle echoed down the phone line. "I've been there." Not that long ago Jack's gut and his fiancée's tenaciousness had been the only things standing between innocent lives and a ruthless serial killer.

"It's not exactly helping matters that I've got a bit of a history with the current camp director, Nicky, and it's not pretty. We had a thing back in the day, and I'm not proud of how it ended." Luke ran his hand over the back of his neck. "I still don't know why it mattered so much to George that I came up this weekend." There were five new vehicles in the parking lot now. Even from a distance he could spot a few familiar faces, including a local politician. "Tabitha Grey just arrived."

Jack chuckled. "Hoping for a weekend of glamor camping no doubt."

Luke grinned. Tabitha was striking woman in her late fifties, with a mane of stylishly coifed red hair. She was with a curvy, much younger woman with the same flame red hair. The younger woman pulled two bags from their trunk. Tabitha's teenaged daughter perhaps?

A large man with a huge white handlebar moustache stepped out of an old pickup with Lake Huron Sports on the side—owner Russ Tusk, probably. There was also a man with a battered fedora whose face he couldn't see, and two young men with huge mops of brown curly hair—twins by the look of it. Then a large blue van with a grizzly bear on the side pulled in. "Big Bear Construction is here, too."

Torchlight News had a pile of unproved allegations about Frances "Bear" Wane's shady dealings and illegal shenanigans almost three inches thick. But with the exception of one dismissed lawsuit where he allegedly waved a handgun at his workers, *Torchlight* had never managed to dig up enough concrete proof to run the story.

"I'm guessing I've got about twenty minutes before I've got to get down there," Luke added. "Last thing I want is Nicky thinking I've bailed on her again. Then I've got no internet or phone until Sunday. Can you do

me a favor and get someone at *Torchlight* to text me
any background I should know about Tabitha Grey,
Russ Tusk of Lake Huron Sports and 'Bear' of Big
Bear Construction?"

"I'm on it."

A breeze rustled the trees behind him. A suspicion
nagged at the back of his mind. "For that matter, Nicky
obviously doesn't like the owner of Ace Sports Resort, Neil Pryce, and the only other person I know was
around the camp is George's son, Trevor Dale."

"Got it." Keyboard keys clicked furiously. "So
you're still going on the camping trip?"

"I'm not even sure I have a choice." Luke said.
"George asked me to and somebody needs to have
Nicky's back." *Whether she likes it or not.* "If it were
up to me, they'd either cancel this trip or send along
some kind of security or police. I don't have your inves-
tigative skills. I'm just a sport's reporter." Not to mention a former runaway with a history of petty crime.
Being back in the local police station last night had
stirred up some uncomfortable memories.

Jack snorted. "Yeah, yeah, yeah. A sport's guy who
just happens to have razor-sharp reflexes. I keep telling you that you should volunteer to coach something
at the community center—"

"And I keep telling you, I'm the last guy anyone's
going to want as a role model."

"So you say," Jack said. "Just give yourself some
credit. Nicky could do worse than you coming along."

People were leaving the parking lot and following
Nicky and Trevor down the trail to the waterfront. The

young curvy redhead was near the back of the pack. As Luke watched, one of the twins—*black shirt, blue bandanna*—ran past her and pressed something into her hand. She slid it into her bag without even looking at it. No one else had seemed to notice, but Luke had spent enough time on the streets to recognize a hand-off when he saw one.

"Still there?" Jack's voice crackled in his ear.

"Yeah. Sorry. Just thought I saw some kind of hand-off between two of the young ones."

"Drugs?"

He rolled his jaw. "Really hope not."

"You want my advice?" Jack said. "Go camping, keep your eyes open and don't stop praying. Trust that if God wants you to see something, or do something, you'll know."

Luke picked up his rucksack and prayed. *Dear Lord, please may he be right.*

The smell of the forest hung heavy in the air and mingled with the scent of ashes. The lodge's hollowed-out shell stood like a shadow behind the beach. Nicky tucked a defiant wisp of brown hair back into her bun and jabbed it down hard with a bobby pin. Every one of the potential donors had arrived—except Luke. Well, if he didn't show, that was on him. The last thing she was going to do was waste another moment of her life waiting around for him.

She watched as Trevor fitted the men and women with life jackets and then showed them how to find the right size paddle. Boney knees jutted out from under

Trevor's plaid shorts as if his joints were trying to escape through his skin, and there was too much gel in
his white-blond hair. But his lanky stance and tone
was so much like George's it was uncanny. She'd never
known the young man to be so thorough. Maybe his
dad being in the hospital had kicked some sense into
him. After all, he had come to rescue her last night.

A tall shadow fell over the path. A smile crossed
her lips. She turned, expecting to see Luke. It was
Neil. Ace Sport's director sauntered down the beach
in between Trevor and the potential sponsors, smiling
and nodding at each one as he went. "Please don't let
me interrupt."

Trevor hesitated then went back to talking about
canoe safety. Neil sidled up behind her. His fingertips
slid over the edge of her clipboards and down over the
list of campers. He whistled softly. "Wow, that's quite
a turnout. Russ Tusk is one of our favorite gear sup-
pliers. Bear Wanes is building a new gym for us this
year. Even Tabitha Grey! You know she cut the ribbon
at the opening of our new pool? I'm guessing the twins
would be David and Aaron Elliot of Up Start? That's
a website that helps young people find volunteer and
job opportunities, right?"

Nicky turned her clipboard over. "What do you
want?"

One hand slid on her shoulder. He pulled her back
a couple of steps away from the group. "Just here to
see if you need anything, doll."

She snorted and shrugged him off. Yeah, as if she
was about to fall for his nonsense today.

The rival camp director raised both hands. "Hey, I just figured that with George in the hospital and your camp locked down, you might appreciate a spare pair of hands this weekend. I can be pretty handy, you know. Come on, we both know Trevor is an all right guy to have a good time with, but he's hardly the kind of solid camp professional you need for a trip like this."

Her back stiffened. True, Neil was hardly telling her something she hadn't thought herself more times than she could count. But she'd take Trevor's laziness and unreliability over Neil's slimy attempts to weasel his way into this trip and steal their sponsors any day. "Spoken like a true 'Acer.' Either someone's the best or they're worthless."

"Look, all joking and rivalry aside, you are a solid camp instructor, Nicky. With skills like yours…" Neil shook his head. "Off the record, you're more than qualified to be a member of Ace Sports' staff team. You know how rare that is for me to admit about anyone."

Did he actually mean that as a *compliment*? Telling her she was good enough for his shiny, obnoxious camp? As if she'd ever doubted she was every bit the athlete as those sparkly, spandex-clad gym nuts that Ace filled its ranks with each summer.

"Our facilities rival any camp in the continent," he went on. "And you know, when it comes to campers, we attract some of the best, most talented young people from across the country…"

She tossed her head. "Wow, you must be desperate to derail our sponsorship trip if you're trying to tempt me to quit just as we're about to set sail. But fortunately for all those campers who aren't up to your stellar standards, not to mention not having Ace Sports' kind of money, Camp Spirit has always been happy to take on people who still need a little work and don't see their ability to toss a ball as something to laud over others."

Neil stepped back. "Believe it or not, I'm actually trying to help you. I'm not going to apologize for being the only one in your life man enough to point out that you're too good for a ragtag place like this." His eyes narrowed. "I just hope that you're smart enough to face the facts before an old man's dying dream ends up dragging you down with it."

SIX

Nicky's fingers tightened on the clipboard. Her heart pounded. What on earth did Neil mean by that? Did he actually know something about George's plans for Camp Spirit she didn't? Or was he just trying to throw her off her game?

"Is that a threat?"

The rival camp director grinned. His hand slid onto her arm. Footsteps pounded down the path. She turned. Luke was jogging through the trees. Her heart skipped an unexpected beat. Looked as if the sports reporter was coming, after all. He looked hard in their direction. An unspoken question flickered in his eyes.

Neil pulled his hand away. "Not a threat, sweetie. Just a cautious word of advice." He nodded to Luke, waved at her campers, then sauntered up the path.

Two hours later Nicky sat alone in the last canoe as they glided in near silence along the wooded shoreline. A few more minutes and she'd be able to point out the hazy outline of the island in the distance. Trevor had gone on ahead in what was now Camp Spirit's only motorboat, loaded down with their packs and equipment. She closed her eyes and listened to the gentle rhythm of paddles dipping in and out of the water. *Lord, I wish George could be here. Help me to inspire these people to pitch in and help keep our camp alive.*

A breeze tickled the base of her neck. She opened her eyes. As much as she wanted to tell herself that Neil had just been tossing around empty words, his tone had hardly sounded like idle smack talk. Of course she knew how fragile the state of Camp Spirit's finances were. She was camp director, not some doe-eyed counselor fresh off the bus. And, yes, unless Trevor's recent responsible transformation stuck, when he inherited the camp, she'd probably be out of a job. But, so what if saving the camp was like trying to patch up a snowman as the spring grew closer? She'd cut her salary down to bare room and board if that's what it took to keep the camp alive even one more year.

She scanned the row of canoes. Tabitha Grey had volunteered to paddle the lead canoe. So much for thinking the politician's icy reputation and poster-ready smile meant she wasn't ready to hack the great outdoors. Tabitha's daughter, Gracie, shared her canoe. A shy girl, Gracie was the baby of the group—five feet tall, full-figured and barely nineteen, with long red hair and a gaze that seemed to constantly drag her eyes toward the identical twin brothers from Start Up.

David and Aaron Elliot were twenty-one. The college students had founded an ambitious youth employment and volunteering website a little over a year ago. It looked as if Gracie's eyes favored older brother

David. But younger brother Aaron was the only one who glanced back her way. *Ah, young people and their crushes.* Then Nicky's gaze fell on the dark, chiseled form of Luke, paddling steadily in the canoe behind them. Strong muscles rippled through his soft gray T-shirt. Her heart fluttered, like a spider skittering through the cobwebs of long-forgotten pathways. She looked away.

Luke was paddling with Martin Bright, who was on the board of directors of a charity called Faith Camps. Martin was a good man. Which was something she couldn't say about the two men paddling to his left. Sports equipment powerhouse Russ Tusk had a white handlebar moustache and the tendency to ooze just a little too much charm. While "Bear" Wanes was a grizzled, brick-shaped man, with the habit of barging into the camp office without an appointment and trying to push George into spending money they didn't have.

A row of swanky hotels and rental chalets rose from a peninsula ahead of them. The loud tinny chimes of a cell phone text split the peaceful air. Paddles fell as hands rose instinctively to people's pockets. Someone must have picked up a momentary signal blip from one of the nearby hotels. But who'd be thoughtless enough to bring a phone after she'd explicitly told them to leave all electronic devices back in their cars? A second text chimed. Then a third and a fourth.

Luke fumbled with his cell phone. She nearly growled. *Of course.* He hadn't respected her then and he apparently still didn't respect her now. She let her eyes roll over the waters. No one was going to knock her off her game. Not a fire. Not a hunter. Not the slimy director of the camp next door. Not even the one man who had once broken her heart.

Even with the sun beating down on his back, Luke could practically feel Nicky's chilly glare floating across the water toward him. If looks could kill, he'd be halfway to the bottom of the lake by now. Was it too much to ask that she actually have some faith in him? Or had the foolish lies he'd told as a teenager ruined any chance of that for good? It would be nice to think she'd actually manage to genuinely smile at the sight of him one day, instead of scrunching up that freckled nose of hers as though she'd just smelled something terrible. He sighed. Didn't help one bit that she still managed to be beautiful when angry.

He glanced at his phone. The cell signal was gone again, leaving four messages in his inbox and the notice that there were two more that hadn't made it through. He read them quickly.

Okay. Pooled the team. Neil Pryce is clean. Unless you count getting kicked out of football minor leagues for breaking someone's nose.

Luke chuckled. No surprise there really.

Tabitha Grey. Politician. Former nurse. Widow. Conservative. Tough as nails. Some angry ex-staff. No scandals. Got nothing on daughter Gracie or what hand-off could've been.

Okay, then. Luke had already figured out it had been the younger twin, Aaron, who'd slipped something into Gracie's hand. And that Gracie had a pretty heavy-duty crush on David.

Russ Tusk. Two ex-wives. Three lawsuits for sexual harassment, all settled out of court. Rumors of infidelity. General gossip. No actual news—that we'd report anyway.

Bear Wanes. Big file. But no one willing to go on record. Rumors of shoddy deals, aggressive negotiating tactics, intimidation, threats, extortion, destruction of property, alcoholism, accidental discharge of a firearm, including shooting a gun through someone's office wall. Not to mention—

The text cut off. Luke almost found himself shaking his phone, willing more words to float onto the screen. Seemed whatever else Jack had wanted to say was lost in cyberspace. For a moment he let his eyes linger on Bear and Tusk. The two men seemed in an unspoken competition to each do as little paddling as possible.

Lord, if there's something You need me to see to there, please help me see it.

The island was even more beautiful in sunlight. Towering pines rose thick and dense out of solid gray rock, like a natural fortress emerging from the water. There was no telling what someone would pay for the rugged, isolated slice of paradise. Luke's paddle froze in his hands. A shadowy green figure stood on the same giant rock where he and Nicky had watched the Hunter peel off in their stolen motorboat the night before. Instinctively, Luke's legs almost pushed him up to his feet before he could even register that he was still in a canoe. "Nicky!"

Nicky waved both arms at the figure on the cliff. He waved back then disappeared into the woods. "Sorry, just had to let Trevor know we saw him. Now what's up?"

Luke fought the urge to smack himself with a paddle. *Of course.* The entire convoy had practically come to a standstill now. Every pair of eyes was on his face. He forced a smile. "Sorry. I just thought that was our visitor from yesterday."

"Nope, we're all good. It's Trevor."

How could she even tell that for sure from this distance? But if it had been the Hunter, he probably wouldn't have waved. Then again, sitting on the lake with a bunch of other canoers, Luke was hardly in a position to argue. Nicky turned back and continued paddling. The canoes fell into formation.

"Hey, can people dive off that rock?" It was the older twin, David.

A glimmer of a smile crossed Nicky's lips. "We don't allow it. The water is pretty deep, but there are a whole lot of other smaller rocks to dodge on the way down."

"But is it possible?" David didn't sound like the kind of guy who liked taking no for an answer.

Now was he reckless, arrogant or brave?

"Only one staffer has ever been foolish enough to

try," Nicky said. "Fortunately she survived with nothing worse than a couple of stitches. But the moment George found out about it, he threatened to fire her if she ever pulled a stunt that dangerous again."

"Was it you?" David asked.

She opened her mouth and then shut it again as a blush brushed over her cheeks. "Yes. But don't follow my example, okay?"

David guffawed loudly. Others chuckled. Aaron smiled weakly at Gracie. But her eyes were too focused on David to notice. The canoes kept moving.

Trevor was waiting for them on the dock, beside the motorboat. His reflective yellow jacket practically glared like a spotlight in the sun. "Welcome everyone to our island!" Trevor spread his arms wide. "Now, please beach your canoes over there on the sand."

He hopped off the dock into knee-deep water and helped drag canoes up onto the shore. Trevor grinned at Luke. "Saw Dad quickly at the hospital this morning, and he said I should get to know you." He guided Luke and Martin's canoe up into the beach beside Bear and Russ's. "Sorry I didn't quite recognize you when I picked you and Nicky up from the island last night. I thought you were just some reporter."

Which meant what exactly? Trevor couldn't have been more than ten or eleven when his father had driven Luke to the local jail, then stood there waiting as he'd stammered out his crimes to the officer. Did Trevor remember those nights a teenaged Luke had detoxed from drugs on his sofa? Or had George told him? Either way, it seemed neither of them had told Nicky.

"I *am* just a reporter." Luke managed a smile. "I didn't think you'd ever remember meeting me."

"You're kidding!" Trevor's smile tightened. "You were my dad's favorite prodigal project! When you moved up from just stacking boxes at that paper up to an actual reporting job, Dad was so proud he stuck the article on the fridge."

Before Luke could answer, Trevor ran over to the next canoe. What was he trying to say? That George was *proud* of him for somehow managing to be a less terrible human being than he used to be? Luke shrugged, wanting to shake off the misplaced praise like an invisible coat he had no business wearing.

Nicky led the group of campers single file through the forest. Luke took up the rear, his mind still spinning from Trevor's words. George was wrong about him. Always had been. He'd lost track of the number of times George had asked him to come up to camp because campers "needed a role model" like him.

Luke slapped a tree branch out of his face. Didn't George understand? He wasn't anyone's role model. He was nothing but the wreckage that resulted when a criminally selfish boy took advantage of an extremely drunk girl at some miserable party and then left her all alone to raise the son she obviously wanted nothing to do with. There was nothing laudable about simply being a more decent person than who he'd been raised to be.

Nicky's laughter trickled through the dense trees ahead of him and his face lifted toward it. Had loyalty to George really been the only thing that had brought him up here this weekend? It's not as if he'd expected Nicky to still be here, waiting where he'd left her. Still, he had to admit, the news his buddy Jack had finally found a woman he wanted to create a life with had sent Luke's mind slipping back to the beautiful woman he'd once left among the Muskoka trees. But that was different. Jack might have taken on both a serial killer and his career to be with his Meg. But for Jack, the monster hadn't been inside him. For Luke, it was in the very DNA flowing through his veins.

He'd almost lost sight of the group and was down to just catching the occasional glimpse of Trevor's back through the trees. George's son had taken off his ridiculous yellow jacket and tied it around his waist. It bunched in the back as he walked. No, there was an actual lump under Trevor's shirt. Luke blinked. Now that was a shape a former runaway would recognize anywhere.

"Hold up." Luke hurried forward a couple of steps and tapped Trevor on the shoulder. The rest of the group walked on without them. Luke lowered his voice. "Why are you carrying a concealed weapon?"

Trevor shrugged. "I don't know what you're talking about."

"Yeah, you do. You've got something tucked into the back of your shirt and the only people I've known to carry things like that are trying to hide something." And not something innocent. "Look, I'm not accusing you of anything. But I know you're carrying something, and I want you to know that you can trust me."

Trevor's lips twisted into a smirk, as though he was

trying to decide whether or not to take Luke seriously. Then he shrugged, chuckled and kept walking.

Right, as if Luke was going to let anyone go after a response like that one. With one hand he grabbed Trevor by the shoulder and spun him around. With the other he yanked up the back of Trevor's shirt and grabbed the weapon.

It was a hunting knife.

SEVEN

Nicky and the campers had barely reached the campground when she heard Trevor shout. She looked back. Where had he gone? And for that matter, *where was Luke*? She forced a smile and turned to the group. "If you could all please find your bags, and pick a buddy or two to share a tent with, I'm just going to go check on what's keeping the others."

She walked back to the path as quickly as she could without looking suspicious. Then once she hit the trees she started to sprint. The muffled sound of Trevor spitting out swearwords filtered through the trees. She still couldn't hear Luke. She rounded a corner on the path and her eyes saw a sight her brain didn't even know how to process. Luke had Trevor pinned against a tree. Trevor was swearing and swinging punches.

"What on earth is going on here? Luke! Let him go. Now."

Luke stepped back, his hands out in front of him, as if he was expecting Trevor to charge. Trevor's eyes flashed like he was ready to leap for Luke's throat. But instead, all he did was spit on the ground and mutter one final curse word under his breath.

They were unbelievable. "I'll ask you again, what's going on here?"

Luke straightened his sweaty shirt over his abs. Then he reached down and picked a jagged hunting knife up off the ground. "I caught Trevor carrying this."

"It's not mine!" Trevor pushed between Luke and Nicky. "I was going to tell you about it, and he jumped me."

A harsh laugh crossed Luke's lips that sounded more like a snarl. "I asked you about it and you laughed me off."

"Since when do I answer to you?" Trevor turned his back on Luke. "Nicky, it fell out of someone's bags when I was transporting them over here. I found it in the bottom of the boat and figured the smartest thing to do was keep it hidden until you and I could talk about it privately."

Nicky gasped. "Whose bag?"

"I don't know. It was just lying on the floor of the boat." Trevor's eyes narrowed. "Could belong to this guy for all I know."

"Or it might not have come from anyone's bag at all." Luke's snarl spread into a dangerous grin. She didn't even want to guess the words Luke was holding back behind his clenched teeth. Then again, the young man she'd once known Luke to be wouldn't have just sworn a blue streak at Trevor; he'd have also broken his nose. Maybe he had changed.

Trevor crossed his arms in front of his chest. "I also found some other pretty interesting stuff in some people's bags, too."

"What?" Nicky's voice rose so high it almost squeaked. "You went through people's bags?"

"Yeah!" Trevor snapped. "Because I'd just found a knife! Who knows what else people might have been hiding?"

Nicky squeezed the back of her neck with both hands. They'd been on the island less than an hour and already she was facing a crisis. Searching through people's bags wasn't just unethical—it could totally jeopardize any of them being willing to give them the help Camp Spirit was counting on. But Trevor wasn't staff she'd hired; he was just here as a favor to his father who was in the hospital. Right now, the most important thing was to deescalate this situation. Discipline could wait.

"What you should have done was come to me first," she said. "We could have handled this like adults and asked people who the knife belonged to. Maybe someone would have come right out and claimed it." Though it was a pretty vicious-looking weapon for a simple camping trip, it wasn't totally beyond the realm of possibility that someone had used it hunting and forgotten it was in their bag.

"Well, I found other things, too." Trevor's body practically quivered with nervous energy. "Bear brought a flask of hard liquor. Smells like whiskey. Bear also has surveyor's maps to the entire area—including this island. I wouldn't be surprised if he only came along because he knows someone planning to make Dad an offer for this place and wants to get a jump on a construction bid. You know as well as I do that this camp might be almost bankrupt, but this land it's built on is worth a lot." True. But that didn't change the fact George wasn't about to sell to a developer. "And Gracie had a letter from Aaron, begging her not to come on this trip because he didn't want her to 'get hurt.' Whatever that means."

She couldn't believe her ears. "Searching for weapons hardly justifies reading someone's personal letter!"

"It wasn't sealed! It was barely even folded."

This was getting worse by the moment. Apparently, Trevor's sense of entitlement had gotten way out of control, and she wasn't looking forward to the conversation she'd have to have with George about it when they got back.

Luke's eyebrows rose. "I saw him hand her something before they got in the canoes. This could be it."

This was the first she was hearing of it. "Where is all this stuff now?"

"I put it all back. Obviously!" Trevor gestured like a man deflecting invisible blows. "Except I dumped most of Russ's alcohol out and then left the cap on the flask loose, so he'd think it spilled out on the way here. Because I figured you didn't actually want someone getting *drunk* on your special camping trip. Unless you'd rather I'd just put it back and leave you to confront him about it." His arms crossed. "Believe it or not, I was actually just trying to help. I want Dad to get the money to fix this dump up even more than you do."

She sighed. "I get that, but you've got to know I can't condone any of this, Trevor. Then again, neither am I going to storm into the campsite and cause a scene. I would like you to take personal responsibility for apologizing to everyone, privately, about looking in their bags. I'll let you sort out how and when that takes place, but I expect it done today." She was still in charge of this trip, whether he liked it or not.

He scowled. "I was trying to help."

"I get that. But that doesn't change the fact that you were in the wrong." She took the knife from Luke's outstretched hand. "We'll see if anyone claims this. Either way I'm locking it in the glove compartment of the motorboat until we get back to shore on Sunday."

Trevor sighed loudly. "I don't have to be here, you know. I stuck around to help. And I don't see why you double guess me but just trust Luke blindly."

A bitter smile rose to her lips. "Believe me, I don't trust Luke blindly. But he's not the one who raided people's bags."

"Well, just so you know, I found a little whittled wood carving in Luke's bag. So for all we know, Luke has a thing for playing with knives."

"Wood carving?" Her feet stopped. She turned to Luke. His face paled. "What kind of wood carving?" As she watched, a pained look filled the gray of his eyes. Her heart leaped in her chest. She knew the answer even before Trevor answered.

"A wolf," Trevor said. "It was a little wooden wolf. Carved out of a piece of a tree branch or something. It's on his key chain. Not particularly well carved. Like the kind of amateur work a kid would've done."

Or a crush-struck eighteen-year-old girl who was just learning to whittle and had spent hours trying to craft the perfect gift for a boy named "Louie" because his name sounded a bit like *loup*, the French word for wolf. She'd never even guessed it was his real last name. Or that he'd keep the carving all these years.

"See, so it makes sense he'd have a knife!" Trevor added. "Ask him! He'll tell you!"

She looked at Luke. But Luke had turned and started toward camp.

Luke slid the heavy canvas tent over the metal poles, feeling his shoulders tighten as Nicky walked behind him. They hadn't spoken a word since they'd returned to camp. Instead, Nicky had leaped right into camp director mode, showing campers how to set up the tents and army cots.

What must she be thinking, knowing he'd kept that wolf she'd carved him all those years ago? The moment she'd handed it to him, shyly, sweetly, as they'd sat side by side on that cliff side was the moment he'd realized it was time to grab whatever he could steal and run. It had gone too far. They'd grown too close.

He'd never hidden anywhere more than two nights at a time before, and here he'd been hiding out in that broken cabin at Camp Spirit almost three weeks. As he'd unwrapped the gift, he'd heard the words, *"Wolf, just like me..."* cross his lips, and realized with a start that he'd just risked admitting his real name. The name of a runaway who had warrants out for his arrest. Not to mention coming within heartbeats of falling so deeply for her that he'd risked getting caught. So he'd hugged her, kissed her and slunk out of her life. But he'd kept the wolf she'd carved him. He'd even hung his keys on it when he'd grown up enough to get an apartment with a door that locked and then a car of his own. It was the closest he could ever come to acknowledging the girl who'd once turned his life upside down.

By late morning the tents were up and Nicky said she'd take anyone who was interested down to try the aquatic obstacle course.

Bear slumped into a chair and complained loudly he'd already done more than enough exercise for one day, no doubt irritated to discover his secret whiskey stash was dry.

David was the first to change into a wetsuit and then tossed one at his brother, Aaron.

In the end, it was Martin, Nicky, the twins and Luke who headed down a different, much thinner and steeper, path through the woods. A narrow stream bubbled along the trail beside them, so close at times the group had to hop stepping stones to walk on the other side.

The obstacle course was a ways down the coast from the beach, set in a deep inlet cove. The shore was a sheer bed of rock. A three-story-tall wooden diving structure stood embedded deep in the granite.

Luke's eyes ran over the course. It started with a rope-ladder climb to the top of the first platform. From there, a row of suspended hanging tires hung like free-swinging stairs down to a second story platform planted deep in the water. The course then turned right in a cobweb of climbing ropes down to a third platform. Then finally, swinging logs formed the final stretch of the obstacle, ending at one last platform and a short swim back to dry land. He gazed at Nicky. "You helped build this?"

A beautiful smile crossed her lips, spreading all the way to her hazel eyes. "I designed it. Outdoor courses like this are a passion of mine. I've built a handful of them around Camp Spirit. I have some really amazing sketches for what I'd create here on the island, too." There was something almost infectious about the passion that lit up her face.

"I'd love to see them sometime," he said. Her gaze met his and he held it for a few beats.

"Thank you." Then she rolled her shoulders back and turned to the group. "Welcome to our obstacle course. Now, a few rules. Only three people on the course at any time, and only one person on each segment. If you fall off, just swim to the next segment and wait for the path ahead to clear. No random swimming around, and heads remain above the surface at all times. Life jackets and wetsuits at all times, no exceptions. This cove is really deep. We don't even let staff dive down without a headlamp, because of seaweed and rocks. Now, everyone just take your time, enjoy the climb, and if you fall, make it a really good splash." More nodding. A few smiles. "Let's go."

David, Nicky and Martin were the first to scale the rope ladder. There was some brief conferring at the top, then David took off climbing from one swinging tire to another. His twin stood back on the shore and watched. Aaron was twitchy. There was no doubt about it. The young man was on edge with that same jittery energy Luke had seen in criminals afraid of getting caught. Tension like that had a certain smell to it, when you knew what you were looking for, and from where he was standing, the cofounder of Start Up practically reeked. "You okay?"

"Yeah, yeah. Yeah… Fine…"

Now there was a lie if he'd ever heard one. "Look, I can tell something's up. Big-time. I don't necessarily have to tell anyone else, if you don't want me to, as long as no one's in danger. You can trust me. But I can't just ignore the fact we're out on an island in the middle of nowhere and you look upset enough to punch someone."

"It's…it's nothing."

"I don't believe you."

"It's…it's personal."

Okay, that he believed. Aaron glanced back over his shoulder again. Luke followed his gaze. Were his eyes playing tricks or was there someone standing by the stream watching them? The shadow disappeared into the trees. Luke's hand touched Aaron's shoulder. "Look, I think you should just—"

A deafening crack spit the air. Luke spun back to the obstacle course just in time to see the platform that Nicky and Martin were standing on lurch toward the water. Wooden pillars shook like cardboard. Tires swung wildly, flinging David's body through the air. Then the obstacle course collapsed into the lake on top of the twin, dragging Nicky and Martin down with it.

EIGHT

It was like watching a craft project getting knocked over by a toddler. Luke's heart leaped into his throat as Nicky, David and Martin disappeared under the pile of debris. He ran for the water's edge. *Save them, Lord!* The prayer had barely formed on his lips when a desperate call for help overtook the air. It was David— terrified and trapped, but thankfully still able to shout. A wall of broken timber blocked his view of most of the cove. There was no sign of Nicky or Martin. Luke dove into the water, swam three strokes and then broke through the surface. In vain his eyes scanned the pile of logs, tires and rope for any signs of life. *Oh, Lord, I don't even know where to start.* "David! I'm coming! Nicky, Martin! Shout if you can here me!"

He glanced back. "Aaron! Can you see them?" But Aaron had sunk to his knees beside the water. His face was pale and eyes were closed. Praying? In shock? Maybe both. "Go get help!" Aaron didn't move. David's shouts grew louder. For a second fear flickered like flames at the corners of Luke's mind, but he couldn't afford to let fear win. *Help me, Lord! I can't do this alone.*

"Luke!" Nicky broke through the surface.

Relief burst through his lungs. She swam toward him. Her dark eyes flashed with a determination and clarity that made him long to pull her into his arms. "Are you okay?"

"Yeah." She gasped in a breath and started treading water. "I'm fine. I jumped free before it hit the surface and landed clean. But Martin's hurt. He landed badly and I think he's sprained his wrist. Thankfully he was wearing a life jacket. I was able to get him to shore on the opposite side of the cove. He'll have a long walk around through the forest, but he's safe." By the looks of things Nicky had ditched her life jacket then swum right under the wreckage. "Do you know where David is?"

Luke shook his head. "No."

Her eyes fluttered closed for barely a second as her lips moved in silent prayer. Then she turned to Aaron, still frozen on the shore. "Aaron! Aaron Elliot! Open your eyes and stand up right now! We need your help!" The twin's eyes snapped open, then he dragged himself to his feet. She pointed toward the woods. "Run back to camp, get Trevor and tell him to bring the first-aid kit, got it?"

Aaron nodded and took off through the trees. Luke was so impressed he fought the urge to whistle. Nicky's voice had been filled with so much certainty he half expected the trees themselves to follow her direction. "How did you get him to do that?"

"After more than a dozen years working at this camp, I've seen more than my fair share of emergencies. You get used to dealing with people freezing up in shock and having to snap them out of it. Also, I don't want him here when we dig out his brother."

David's shouts had stopped. Nicky turned back to the wreckage. Her voice rose. "David, don't worry. We're coming to find you. Just stay calm, okay?" A muffled response came from within the wood. Nicky's hand brushed Luke's. Her voice dropped. "I'm going to have to search underwater. I don't know where in this mess he is."

Luke was already shrugging his arms out of his life jacket. "Don't worry. I'm right behind you."

She glanced to the sky. The sun had dipped behind a cloud, but still the scattered light seemed to illuminate her skin. "Lord, help us." She dove underwater.

He followed. The water was green and murky. His eyes strained to follow the lines of her shape cutting through the water in front of him. But just as he felt his lungs begin to ache, she abruptly changed course and swam straight up into the wreckage. He followed and broke through the surface beside her; nearly bumping his head on the wooden beams above his head.

They treaded water, face-to-face, in a little pocket of air, in between some partially submerged tires and the solid wooden wall of what used to be platform floorboards. For a moment all they could hear was the sounds of their own panting for breath mingling with the creaking wood and lapping water. Then he heard David groan.

"David?" Luke found his voice first. "Can you hear me?"

"Yeah…" David's frightened face came into view through the stack of tires.

"Don't move," Nicky said. "Just stay there and wait for us to come to you. Are you hurt?"

"No, I'm okay." His voice was faint. "At least, I think so. I'm kind of pinned between the tires and the roof, though, and I think my life jacket's caught on something."

"Are you able to get it off?" Nicky asked.

"No. I can't reach my arms up. I don't have any wiggle room."

Luke looked at Nicky. "You okay if I try to shift some of this wood?"

She nodded. "Just be careful."

Luke leaned his weight against a load-bearing tire. The wood creaked. He could probably shift things enough to let David slip out. But would that send the wood collapsing in on them? "How about now?"

David's head bobbed slightly. Then he disappeared out of sight. "Okay, I got the life jacket unzipped. But I can't get my chest out of it. I'm pretty tightly pinned. It's like the ceiling is leaning on me."

Nicky glanced at Luke. Her eyebrows rose. "Just lie still and give us a moment to sort something out. Then we'll get you out of here." She swam closer to Luke until her nose was nearly bumping against his face. Her voice dropped to a whisper. "I don't know if you've noticed, but the ceiling is sinking, and the more he wiggles around, the worse it's going to get. We don't have that much longer before this whole thing falls down on our heads. How strong a swimmer are you?"

His arms and legs were aching and his lungs felt like he'd run a marathon. "Strong enough. What do you need?"

A grim smile crossed her lips. "I can swim underwater to him and cut him out of the life jacket. I've got a small utility knife on me. I'm just afraid that if his body's helping keep this thing afloat, once he moves, the whole thing is going to cave in on top of us."

Luke's jaw set firmly. "You go get him. I'll stay here and hold the ceiling up. Then once you're free from the wreckage, I follow you out."

"But it'll crush you."

"No, it won't. Because I'm a lot bigger than David is and I'll be supporting it with my arms, not my body. All I've got to do is let go and dive down. It's still wood. It's hardly going to drop on top of me like a stone." At least he hoped not. Nicky's face turned toward the shifting wood above. Luke's fingers brushed her cheek. "Don't lose focus. You have to get David out. You're smaller and a more agile swimmer. I'm going to keep this structure afloat just long enough to give you time to do that, because I'm the only one with the upper body strength to do it. That's how it's got to be. Teamwork."

Hazel eyes searched his face. "If things collapse in on you…"

"Then it will hardly be the worst blow I've ever taken. I've got a pretty tough skull. I'll push on through and keep swimming until I join you on dry land." He moved closer still, until she was treading water in between his arms. "You know it's got to be this way."

She took a deep breath. Then nodded. "Okay, but if anything goes wrong I'm going to get you out of here. Even if I've got to yank the planks off you one by one."

"I know you will." His voice grew thick as he felt a surge of emotion push through his words. Her long dark hair fell free, framing the lines of her face, trailing around them in the water and tugging at memories of the very young woman she'd once been. Did she have any idea how much he admired her? How strong a person he knew she was? How he'd always known? "Nicky, I trust you."

The wood above them lurched. A board knocked against his head. They were running out of time. Suddenly he couldn't stop the words tumbling over his lips. "Look, Nicky, I'm sorry again. For the person I used to be. For everything. And no matter what happens I hope you know—"

Her finger brushed over his lips. "Tell me when we're back on dry land." She turned back toward the mass of tires. "Okay, David, it's time we all get out of here. I'm going to swim over right now and cut you loose. Once I do, dive down, follow me and swim out as fast as you can. Don't stop and don't look back. We'll be right behind you. Luke, you ready?"

He flexed his arms. "Ready."

"We got this." Her lips brushed his cheek. "See you on the other side."

She dove. The ceiling was only a few inches above his head now. For a moment silence filled his ears.

Then he heard Nicky shout, "I got him! We're heading out!"

There was a splash. The wood shifted. The ceiling dropped into his hands. The crushing weight nearly knocked him underwater before he was able to push it back up again. Nicky and David were still swimming out. He would not let it fall.

Luke's arms buckled. Wet wood slid beneath his fingers. He arched his back until he could feel the dull ache of the wood above him pressing into his shoulders. He gasped in a breath, his mouth barely an inch above the water.

Please, Lord, he prayed, *help me. I can't let Nicky down. Not this time.*

Then he heard her voice fill the air. "Luke! We're safe!"

"Great. Okay, I'm com—"

His breath was knocked from his lungs as the ceiling caved in on top of him.

NINE

"Luke!" A scream left Nicky's lips as the remains of the obstacle course dropped into the dark green water. She scanned the surface, willing Luke to break through. No bubbles. No movement. No Luke. Was he knocked unconscious? Or trapped underwater, drowning as he struggled to break free? *Please, Lord. Please don't let him die.* The debris creaked and shuddered, then dropped another inch. David was crawling onto the shore but Aaron was yet to return with the others. "Wait here. I'm going back to find him."

She took a deep breath and dove toward the structure. A wall of green filled her eyes. Then she saw the bubbles. Hundreds. Luke was trapped and thrashing, churning the water around him as he battled against whatever was holding him. Her heart lurched. If he didn't stop fighting she wouldn't be able to see how he was stuck or get close enough to help him break free. She paused underwater, for one heart-wrenching second, begging his eyes to turn toward her and see that she was there; begging him to let her save his life.

But all she could see was the uncontrollable fight of a drowning man. Her lungs screamed for air. Her heart ached in prayer. *Oh, God, please! Let him see that I'm here and want to help save him!* With each stroke she could feel her body growing weaker. If she didn't leave soon and swim back for air, she could drown, watching him drown.

Then Luke's eyes fell upon her face. Their blue-gray depths were filled with a mixture of bravery and need that seemed to shatter her aching heart, sending fresh blood filling her veins. Luke stopped fighting. The water cleared. And she could see. His leg was twisted behind him. His foot was tangled in a harness rope tethered to two beams the size of telephone poles.

She swam to him, yanked her knife from her pocket and hacked at the ropes that held him. He kicked back hard and broke free. They swam for the surface. She broke through the water and gasped as air filled her lungs again. Grateful tears rushed to her eyes and poured down her cheeks. Luke grabbed on to a free-floating log, then reached for her hand and pulled her toward it. She hung there, panting.

"You saved my life." Luke's voice dragged her gaze back to his face. The sky above pooled in his unguarded eyes. It was the same way he had looked at her the day before he'd run. Open. As though his eyes were a doorway to his soul and he was inviting her inside, asking her to get to know him better. No wonder she'd given him her heart. She'd believed that he'd actually meant it.

"No problem. You saved mine first. Now we're even."

She'd said it lightly enough. But he didn't smile. Instead, the look in his eyes deepened and darkened with emotions that made her wish there was something a lot stronger than a broken piece of wood between them. His eyes searched her face, her lips, her throat, as if he was tracing them from memory. It was as though he was floating adrift at sea and she was his first fleeting glimpse of land. His index finger brushed against the side of her hand. It was enough to send shivers shooting through her core.

He needed to leave. She needed him off this island, away from her camp and out of her life. Because otherwise he'd just keep chipping away at her heart, bit by bit, glance by glance, until once again she'd find herself falling for someone who was only going to walk off and hurt her again. It didn't matter how intense a look pooled in his eyes, or how deeply she felt it tug at her heart. He'd told her in the caves last night—he hadn't known how to love her and was glad that he'd left her. He did not regret having left her before. It was only a matter of time before he'd hurt her again.

Trevor was running down the path through the woods now, with the others on his heels. "Nicky! Is everyone okay?"

She turned toward the shore. "All safe and accounted for. No signs of obvious major trauma. Martin landed on the other side of the cove and is heading this way through the woods. You need to find him right away and get his arm in a sling. He may have sprained it. We'll get these people some lunch quick, then you're going to need to grab the motorboat and take David, Martin and Luke to get checked out at the hospital."

"Actually, I think I'm okay to stay with the rest of the group," Luke said. "I'm a bit sore, but nothing major."

"Glad to hear it." She didn't even let herself look at him. "But you were trapped underwater just a few moments ago. I think, just to be on the safe side, I'd feel better if you went back with them and got checked out by a doctor. After that, maybe you should consider staying on the mainland until George gets out of the hospital. Don't get me wrong, I appreciate that you wanted to come on this trip, see the island and support what we're trying to do here. But it sounds like George really wanted to talk to you about something, and maybe that should be the highest priority right now."

The words felt heavy on her tongue, almost as though she was betraying something or someone as she said them. But her highest priority right now was to bail out this sinking camp enough to keep it going, even just for a few more years. While someone like Russ could help with sporting goods, Bear could help with construction and David and Aaron could help with volunteers, the only thing she could see Luke contributing was some newspaper article. Press and publicity were nice, but they were hardly the most important thing right now. Besides, floating here, surrounded by wreckage of the course she'd once built, was a stark reminder this whole place was in danger of collapsing around her. The last thing she needed was a distraction like Luke, knocking her off kilter and sending her emotions into chaos.

"Look, it just makes sense," she added. "George is in the same hospital that Trevor is going to be taking you to. You should at least go along, get a five-minute checkup, chat to George if he's got visiting hours, and then decide if you want to come back with Trevor, hang around on the mainland or head back to Toronto."

He looked at her as if she was nothing but a block of carpentry wood he was turning around in his hands. "Nicky? Why are you trying to get rid of me?"

She pressed her lips together. "George was the one who invited you up, not me, and he's on the mainland. It's hardly like you were planning on staying up here more than a couple of days, anyway. Don't get me wrong, I'm really thankful for everything you've done. But I think it would be better for both of us if you just went."

She pushed away from the log and swam for the shore.

Frustration surged through Luke's chest so fiercely he almost laughed. Did Nicky honestly think she could just order him off the island? Yes, he'd come up here as a favor to George. But last he checked, Nicky was the one in danger. It was bad enough that Trevor was now going to be leaving with their only motorboat. Did she believe Luke was just going to pack up and leave her here on the island without any kind of backup?

By the time he caught up with her, Nicky had already climbed back on shore and was in full-fledged camp director mode. The plan was for people to get changed out of their wetsuits, then relocate everyone to the beach and sort out some quick-packed lunches for those going to the hospital, along with sandwiches for those staying behind. She quickly and calmly explained to the group that it would take Trevor about half an hour to get back to camp and another half hour to drive to the hospital, although if anyone needed it, once he got back in cell signal range he could call for an ambulance. If all went well, they'd only be in the hospital for an hour or two. Trevor and the campers who'd gone with him would easily be back on the island in time to join the others for dinner. Unless, of course, anyone chose to stay behind on the mainland.

It all seemed so rational and simple, even reassuring under normal circumstances. Quick ride to the mainland, short hospital visit and back before sunset—no worries. Except for the fact someone might have just tried to kill them. The group split into those Trevor was leading through the woods to the beach and those heading back to the tents to get changed. Luke waited as people filed past. Then his hand touched Nicky's elbow. "You're going to cancel this camping trip, right?"

She stopped in her tracks. "Can you please keep your voice down?"

He had been. Why was she acting like this? Until a few minutes ago it looked as if they had actually started trusting each other, and now she was pushing him away again. He had to admit, he was getting pretty tired of being treated like the bad guy. "Nicky, the obstacle course just collapsed. Someone could have been killed."

Nicky leaned in so close he could almost feel her shoulder brush against his. "Yes, the obstacle course just collapsed, injuring one person and nearly taking out three more. Which is why Trevor is taking people to hospital—"

"And you don't find it suspicious?"

She glanced toward the departing others, then stepped back against a tree. "That an obstacle course just happens to collapse the day after the lodge catches fire? Of course I do. But the whole reason George invited these sponsors up here is that the camp is so cash strapped it's in danger of falling apart."

"So that's what you think, then? That the lodge fire, the dangerous trespasser who stole our boat and now this—" His hand waved over the floating debris. "This is all just some big coincidence?" The words flew out of his mouth so rapid-fire he was practically shooting them out like arrows. But the harsh tone froze on his tongue when he saw tears floating in the depths of her eyes.

"You think I want to believe my camp is in such bad shape it's gotten *dangerous* without my realizing it? Or would I rather believe that the trespasser who threatened me yesterday also decided to sabotage the obstacle course before he stole my boat?" Her shoulders rose and fell, as if admitting defeat.

"In either case, what's our rationale for not staying here a few more hours and limiting ourselves to low-key things like walking and roasting marshmallows?

Even if I did decide to give up and evacuate the island how exactly would I do that? There are *ten* people on this island right now and only four seats in the motorboat. Do I try to convince everyone to leave their gear behind and overload the boat with more people than it can safely handle? Do I make a camp full of already exhausted people pack everything up again and paddle another two-and-a-half hours to dry land?"

She crossed her arms in front of her chest. "You make it sound like I haven't actually been thinking about any of this. This is hardly my first rodeo."

His heart fell. He'd mistaken her composure for callousness. "So, we're stuck between a rock and a hard place."

"Pretty much."

"Then how about instead of shutting me out, you fill me in on what you're thinking, so I can at least back you up?"

"Fair enough." Nicky glanced toward the campers. "Trevor's going to file a police report and brief George. He won't be gone for more than three or four hours. If George wants us to evacuate immediately, Trevor can get one or two of our friends to come along with their boats to take us all back. He may very well bring the police with him, too. Or, George might say we all stay here overnight and paddle home tomorrow. I don't know. Sadly, someone has to stay here with these campers, and that person is me. But if you're really worried about it, how about you go back with Trevor and report it to the police yourself?"

Nice try. He wasn't going anywhere.

TEN

They all gathered on the beach to wave the boat off. Luke hung back by the canoes and watched as Nicky quickly went over new plans. Anyone who wanted to was of course welcome to leave the island now, but if they had more takers than would fit in the motorboat they'd have to either all leave via canoe or wait until the motorboat came back. She offered to give them a few moments to think it over. Then she pulled out the hunting knife, as cool as a spring breeze, and asked if it belonged to anyone. Silence swept across the beach. She waited, nodded and then calmly locked it in the motorboat glove compartment. *Like a pro.*

He couldn't take his eyes off her. She was a natural leader. He found himself searching his mind for any clues the cute and spunky girl who'd once captured his heart as a teenager would grow up to be such a caring, capable camp director. But all he came up with were scattered references to how much she simply loved being at camp, and far too many memories of him cutting her off, to fill the air with dishonest tales of his own. She'd always been a better listener than he knew how to be.

Hey, Lord, he found himself praying, *she was so obviously made for this. Please, sort this whole mess out in some way that she gets to stay camp director of Camp Spirit. Either that or find her something even better.*

In the end Trevor, David, Martin and Tabitha made the trip back to the mainland. A bit surprising that the politician claimed the fourth seat in the boat, as Luke would have expected Aaron would want to stick close to his injured brother, and Tabitha to want to stay on the island with her daughter, Gracie. Or did the politician not notice Gracie seemed to be embroiled in some kind of drama with the twins? But as a former nurse, Tabitha had volunteered to help keep an eye on the injured. Despite Trevor's recent burst of responsibility, Luke also suspected Nicky was secretly grateful to have Tabitha along to keep the trip on track. The last thing they needed was for Trevor to get sidetracked on the mainland and delay coming back.

As the boat pulled away Luke mentally updated his list of who was left on the island. Gracie, the moody college student. Aaron, the twitchy twin with something to hide. Bear, of Big Bear Construction, who was definitely grumpy, probably had a drinking problem and was potentially corrupt. Russ, the rumored ladies' man who sold sporting goods. Himself and Nicky. In one fell swoop their camp of ten was down to six. At least for now.

They all returned to the campsite. Nicky took them

on a gentle walk around a few of the highlights of the island. Then Russ strung a rope between two trees and played a lighthearted game of volleyball with Gracie and Aaron. Bear napped under a tree.

Luke kept an easy-going grin on his face while his reporter's mind watched them each as suspects. But suspects in *what* exactly? Had one of them really tried to sneak a knife onto this trip, been in cahoots with whoever had attacked Nicky last night and stolen their boat, or known something about the damage to the lodge and obstacle course? If so, why? To help a rival camp? To totally devalue how much money George and Trevor would eventually be able to sell the camp for? Because of some personal vendetta against Camp Spirit...or even Nicky?

Every trail Luke could feel his mind racing down seemed to hit a dead end. If George gave up and sold for some cut-rate price, the only people who came away with money in their pockets were him and his son. While Luke hadn't exactly been a fan from what he'd seen of Trevor so far, as Nicky had pointed out, it was only in Trevor's best interest for the camp to succeed financially. It was no surprise he'd offered to come along and help with this trip—if some of these sponsors did invest, Trevor's inheritance would only increase in value.

What they were looking for was someone who wanted the camp ruined, worthless and destroyed. How did a wistful politician's daughter, the nervous half of a youth employment charity or a potentially sleazy sporting good's salesman benefit from that?

While Aaron and Gracie had been behaving oddly, neither of them had given so much as a peep when David had risked his life by climbing up the obstacle course. Also, while the maps in Bear's bags made it even more likely he hoped to score some kind of lucrative construction deal with the land's future buyer, it still didn't explain who that buyer was or prove that Bear would be willing to go to all this trouble for them.

The day wore on. The sun dipped lower and lower until long, golden rays brushed the treetops. Eventually everyone gathered around the campsite, with that kind of restless, idle chatter that comes when people expect to be interrupted. Finally, Nicky started to build a campfire in the fire pit, then started prepping a pot of stew for dinner. Trevor and the others had been gone almost seven hours. Apparently, Trevor was taking his sweet time returning or planning their rescue was taking longer than they'd expected or something had gone terribly wrong.

Luke glanced to the sky. There was probably less than an hour of daylight left. If he wanted to take a closer look at the broken obstacle course before the sun set completely, he'd have to go now. He tossed a backward glance at where Nicky now crouched beside the fire and waved his hand in the direction of the stream. She nodded and he started for the cove.

It was so weird being around her after all these years. Some moments it was as if someone had erased the past decade and they hadn't been apart more than a day. Others, the strength in her shoulders and the lines of her face made her seem like a virtual stranger—so much older and more confident than the young girl he'd left years ago.

Instinctively his fingers felt for his key chain, before forgetting he'd left it tucked safely in his bag. The wolf she'd once carved for him had long been smoothed over by the rhythmic rub of his fingers as he felt for his keys, or simply stroked it in the kind of mindless way another man might otherwise have tapped his fingers. He never felt fully dressed without it in his pocket.

Nicky was like a box that he'd dumped his heart and soul into then buried somewhere, never expecting to see it unearthed. Despite his best attempts at dishonesty, it was funny just how much real stuff he'd managed to spill out into her hands. Here, she was convinced he was nothing but a liar because all the facts had been invented. But as for his emotions—his fears, doubts, longings and hopes—he'd been more honest with her than he'd been with anyone before. Maybe even since.

The sky was dark blue above the lake. The deep cold waters of the cove looked almost black. The wooden remains of the fallen diving tower lay half submerged like a fossil receding slowly into the mud. His eyes ran over the remains with the precision of a sports journalist—calculating possible angles and trajectories, examining splintered beams and broken poles, with the same skill and precision he'd use to map out how to swing a bat or shoot a hockey puck.

The biggest tower, the one set inside the cove, had collapsed into the water just before David had gotten there. The weight of it had apparently dragged the rest of the course down with it. This meant that whatever evidence had made the structure fall was now under water, being washed away or sinking deeper into the mud. It would be impossible to lift fingerprints when the crime scene was underwater.

A dark orange glow was creeping into the hazy outline of the very distant shoreline. Long rays sent shadows dancing on the water. A breeze brushed the trees and movement caught his eye. Something was sticking out of the wooden wreckage of the fallen tower. Bright yellow and neon green. It was fluttering.

Luke kicked off his shoes and dove cleanly into the lake, feeling the water seep into his T-shirt and jeans. He broke through the surface and shivered. If he'd realized there was a chance he'd go swimming he'd have brought a wetsuit. His body cut through the water, dodging the underwater obstacle course of tattered ropes and broken wood. He reached the splintered base of what was once a tower and a growl filled his throat.

One of the Hunter's arrows was imbedded in the top.

"What are you doing?" The words flew from Nicky's mouth even before her feet reached the water's edge.

Luke was swimming in the middle of the cove, surrounded by broken wood and debris on all sides. This man was unbelievable.

Luke treaded water. "I found something you've got to see." He pulled off his T-shirt, wrapped it around his hand and tried to yank something from the wood. He sighed. "It's another titanium hunting arrow. Exactly like the one you found yesterday. But it's in pretty deep and I can't get it out of the wood without breaking it."

A painful breath filled her lungs. The Hunter was back, and he'd fired an arrow into the obstacle course. As a calling card or as a warning?

Luke swam back, holding his shirt in his hands. "I'm going to leave it there. I don't want to risk breaking it and ruining potential evidence." He reached the rocky shore and pulled himself up. Water streamed off his muscles and flowed over his childhood scars, his skin bronze in the dying light. Her eyes traced from the intensity in his eyes down the strong lines of his jaw. His teeth were clenched.

She swallowed hard. "Any chance the arrow was there before the tower toppled and we just didn't see it?"

He ran both hands through his hair. "Nope. It was clear through the top of a broken pillar. It was definitely fired sometime between when we all left the cove and when I got back here ten minutes ago."

A shiver ran down her spine. While she'd been casually showing the few remaining sponsors around the island, the same man who'd held a knife to her throat barely twenty-four hours ago had shot an arrow into the wreckage of the course that had nearly drowned them.

"So, he's still here on the island and he's toying with us." The words slipped over her lips as barely more than a whisper. For a moment she felt so helpless that hot tears rushed to her eyes.

Luke spread his arms wide to make room for her. She stepped between them until the comforting strength of his chest pressed up against hers. Her hands dropped down at her sides even as she fought the urge to let them creep up around his neck. He brushed the fingers of one hand lightly along her arm, making her crave an emotional intimacy with him that she knew she'd never have.

She stepped back. People were counting on her. The besotted girl who had once fallen into Luke's loving arms was now long gone. And he was the only person on this island she knew for sure she could depend on to help get everyone else back safely.

"So, the Hunter came back after stealing our boat yesterday. We never did find where he hid his boat. Maybe he needed to come back for it. Either that or he somehow snuck onto the island sometime today."

"Or he might be one of the four people back at the campsite right now," Luke said. "I don't know about you, but I didn't have eyes on Aaron, Gracie, Russ and Bear the whole day. It's possible one of them snuck away, came down here and fired this arrow. Either because they are the Hunter or they're working with him for some reason."

Something rustled in the forest behind them. They both spun sharply. She searched the tree line. But she couldn't hear anything but the whispers of trees in the afternoon breeze. The Hunter could be anywhere. Lurking behind any tree. Silent. Deadly. Considering how far a high-tech bow like his could shoot, the campers wouldn't be any safer sitting in the canoes on open water than they would be at the campsite. Nowhere was safe anymore. *Lord, please bring Trevor back soon and with reinforcements.*

"We don't have any choice," Nicky said. "I'm going back to camp to make sure everyone has a good, solid dinner in them. The stew's cooked, so we might as well eat it and get our strength up, instead of trying to get out of here on an empty stomach. When we've eaten, we're going to pack up and paddle out of here. Just because no one's been seriously hurt by the Hunter's antics so far doesn't mean I'm about to take the risk his next stunt won't be fatal.

"As much as I hate the idea of asking people to risk the danger of canoeing at night, we have flashlights. I don't know what's taking Trevor so long. I'd much rather we rendezvous with Trevor on the open water twenty minutes after leaving here than risk us having to spend the night."

"Agreed," Luke said, pulling his wet T-shirt on.

Slowly they made their way upstream, toward the campsite. Trees whispered around them. The ground cover rustled beneath their feet.

She couldn't shake the feeling they were being watched. "I hate the idea that one of those four people I left back at camp could be behind this—or part of it, anyway. For all I know, I'm about to ask the hunter himself to climb in a canoe with me. But I'm not about to leave potentially innocent people behind either."

Luke's face was grim. "You know, we keep saying 'he' but it could have been anyone in those fatigues. Those things were huge enough to mask almost anyone's shape, and you don't need that much strength or power when you've got a two-thousand-dollar high-tech bow on your side. Bows like that even come with scopes to make sure you hit your target."

"Well, it can't be Gracie," Nicky said. "She's the only one I'm convinced couldn't have attacked me. Not because she's a girl, but because she's too short and I'm pretty confident I could overpower her pretty easily. Bear's just too huge. I'd have known if that much weight was pressing into me. But that doesn't mean either of them can't be working with whoever attacked me yesterday. I'm not even sure Aaron could successfully get the jump on me, even though the Hunter did have the advantage of surprise. Not that learning Aaron tried to warn Gracie off coming here doesn't worry me silly, especially coupled with how blatant it is she'd do just about anything for David."

She ran her hands over her arms. "You know, if I ever caught one of my counselors staring at a guy the way she looks at him, I'd be bringing her into my office for a heart-to-heart on the dangers of liking a guy so much you give up your own self-esteem. In fact, the most compelling evidence that Gracie had nothing to do with the course falling is that David was on it."

"Which just leaves Russ," Luke said.

"Who could have been in those fatigues, yeah." Nicky shoved a branch out of her way. "But as far as I'm concerned, both Russ and Bear are worth worrying about. Suddenly your theory that Neil at Ace Sports might be involved doesn't seem as silly as I thought. Bear built every single one of Ace's big shiny buildings and Russ is on Neil's bowling team."

The ground sloped steeply upward. Her heart weighed heavy in her chest. "It's going to kill George to see his camp go down in flames like this, and whoever's doing this is basically robbing Trevor of his inheritance, too. I can't imagine anyone hating the Dales enough to do this to their family."

A panicked cry filtered through the trees. Nicky grabbed Luke's arm as the screams grew louder.

Gracie was pleading for help.

ELEVEN

Nicky sprinted through the trees, Luke on her heels, as Gracie's high-pitched screams echoed through the forest. "Hang on! We're coming!"

They burst into a clearing, nearly falling onto the fight unfolding in front of them. Gracie was standing, shaking, eyes wide, hands pressed to her lips, as Russ threw Aaron up against a rock. Russ pulled back his fist, prepared to plunge the full force of his weight into the younger man's jaw.

"Stop it! Now!" Nicky could hear her own voice echo, as if coming from somewhere outside herself.

Luke lunged, grabbed Russ's arm and yanked it back. Aaron crumpled to the ground and Gracie tumbled down onto the dirt beside him.

Russ swore loudly. "Let me go."

Luke held him firm. "Not until I know you're not going to hit anyone."

"You kidding me?" Russ was practically foaming at the mouth. "I was defending myself. That little twerp jumped me!"

Luke glanced at Nicky. She nodded. Luke let Russ go, but kept his hands in the air, just inches away from the man. Nicky let out a long breath mingled with prayer. *God, I'm sorry I ever griped about You sending Luke along on this trip. I don't want to guess how I would have pulled these two men apart without him here.*

Aaron wiped a drop of blood off his lips. "He attacked Gracie. I was just defending her." He wrapped a protective arm around the girl's shoulders.

Russ's face grew red. "I did nothing of the sort. She looked sad. Upset, like she was about to cry, you know? So I just gave her a hug and she got all hysterical. Typical overly emotional woman."

"He grabbed me from behind." Gracie's voice was quiet, but Nicky could almost hear Tabitha's strength moving through her daughter's words.

Russ spluttered and spun back toward the couple as if ready to hit whichever one flinched first.

Nicky stepped in front of them, without even glancing at the fist hovering inches from her face. "Is that true?"

Russ snorted. Then he looked at Luke as if she wasn't even there. "That girl is lying. I just hugged her. She was looking sad. Her mom isn't back yet. So I walked up and I gave her a hug. Since when is that a crime?"

Yeah, Nicky had seen enough young, female counselors duck Russ's unwanted, impromptu hugs that she could guess how that had gone. He'd known better than to ever try it with her. "You hugged her from behind and without asking her."

"So what? That boy's the criminal who jumped me. I should have him arrested."

Right, as if Russ would risk the damage to his reputation a court case would cause.

"Aaron was just protecting me!" Gracie's voice rose. "He didn't even hit you. He just tried to pull you off me!"

"He threatened to kill me!"

"He didn't mean it! He was just trying to get you to stop!"

Nicky held up a hand. "Is that true Aaron?"

Aaron nodded. "Yeah. Close enough. I didn't hurt him. But he'd have deserved it if I did. He was trying to take advantage of her." Aaron's arm tightened protectively around Gracie. The gesture was almost brotherly.

"See!" Russ jabbed his hand in their direction.

Nicky squared her shoulders. "Russ, you owe Gracie an apology. Whether you meant to or not, you scared her pretty badly. Not that Aaron was justified in threatening you, if he did…

"The stew should be about finished. I suggest we all head back to camp and take a few moments to calm down. Once we're no longer running on empty stomachs, we're going to pack up camp and head back to the mainland. Hopefully, Trevor will be back by then. If not, we're going to canoe it. Feel free to head to the police station and report this incident when we all get back. In the meantime, I suggest everyone take a few deep breaths and try to calm down."

"So the camp mommy is trying to tell me to apologize and try a time-out?" Russ spluttered a laugh that was more like a bark. Once again, his words were directed straight at Luke. "I can't believe what I'm hearing. You going to just stand there like a moppet and let her call the shots?"

Luke's angry grin stopped just short of a snarl. "Yeah, I am. It would do you good to remember that Nicky is the boss of the place and we're here as her guests."

Russ let out a string of swearwords that was more shout than understandable syllables. His fat finger waved in front of Nicky's nose. "You think a little girl like you can tell me what to do? You need someone to teach you a lesson." Then he stepped back and swung his arms wide. "As for this camp? It can fall apart and rot. The moment I get back to my office, I'm tearing up every single one of our contracts for this summer. Then I'm going to march into that hospital room and tell that old geezer George that until he sees some sense, fires you and puts a real man in charge of this place, my company will never do business with him or Camp Spirit ever again. Good luck finding enough paddles and life jackets to stay afloat now." He turned toward the trees. "Yeah, I'm going to go get my bag. And then I'm going to grab whichever canoe I want—canoes that *I* sold you—and paddle myself back to shore."

"No one should be going anywhere alone right now." She could rise above Russ's rudeness. But that didn't mean she was about to let him go charging alone through the woods without a warning. "We now think there might be a trespasser on the island and he's armed with hunting arrows. We think he might have intentionally sabotaged the obstacle course. I don't know if anyone's in actual danger, otherwise we wouldn't have waited this long for the motorboat to come back. But we'd rather not risk having anyone go running off alone."

Russ snorted. "I'd like to see anyone try to stop me."

A bright fire crackled in the stone pit in front of Luke. Behind him, only two tents were still left standing. The others had been packed and rolled, and were now lying in a pile of equipment waiting to be shipped back to shore. A half-empty stew bowl lay by his feet.

Luke's watch beeped. He glanced down. Eight o'clock at night. It was hard to believe any son of George's could be this flaky and unreliable. Then again, maybe Trevor just didn't want to face the music about having gone rummaging through people's bags, so was now sulking in some bar on the mainland. Either way, Luke was rapidly losing both respect and patience for him.

Luke hadn't seen Russ since the man had shoved his things into a bag and charged off through the woods like a rhinoceros. Luke had made one final attempt to stop him, but Russ had been too angry to listen and Luke wasn't about to physically attack the man just to keep him from canoeing alone.

Now just five of them remained around the campfire. Aaron and Gracie sat side by side on a log to his right. Aaron was eating. Gracie just turned a hunk of bread around in her hands, barely nibbling at the edges.

As for getting home, they now had bigger problems. Bear sat on the other side of the fire pit, a wobbly grin on his face. He stank of alcohol. It appeared that on top of the flask Trevor had found in his bag, there'd also been one stashed in his pockets. While Luke and Nicky had been in the woods, first inspecting the obstacle course and then trying to calm the conflict between the others, Bear had managed to get enough hard liquor into himself that he was too drunk to walk without staggering.

Great. Now they had one camper both furious and missing, and another too drunk to safely risk getting into a boat. Hopefully that was the only thing someone had managed to smuggle onto the island.

Luke's eyelids felt heavy. He let them close for a moment as he muttered a prayer under his breath. *Dear Lord, now what?* Then he felt the weight shift under him. He opened his eyes. Nicky had dropped down beside him on the log. "How are you holding up?"

She shrugged, her gaze lost deep inside the burning fire. Firelight danced across her skin, sending dark shadows down the lines of her throat. There was almost something ethereal about her. Nicky was this odd, unexplainable combination of both fierce strength and aching vulnerability—and the most beautiful thing he'd ever seen.

"I'm okay." She sighed softly. "Not much we can do. I'd just managed to get my head around getting everyone to canoe home safely after dark. I never factored in maneuvering a huge drunk into a canoe with us."

"We could wait until he passes out," Luke suggested, "then I could take him alone in a canoe with me. That way if he woke up suddenly, flailed around and capsized the boat, I'm the only one in danger."

Nicky shook her head. "He could take off his life jacket or hit his head and drown. Besides, I'm not about to risk your life, either." She leaned into his side. The back of her hand bumped against his. "Right now, I just have to hope that Russ makes it back safely and that Trevor's delay is nothing more serious than his usual, unreliable self-centeredness." Her body nestled even closer into his. Then her head drooped so low that her forehead landed on his shoulder. "Just promise me you're not about to run off without me this time."

"What?" He tilted her face up toward him. "Of course I'd never leave you alone here in danger. I'm sticking as close to you as I can until everyone's home safely. That's a promise."

Dark, haunted eyes looked up into his. She looked ready to fall asleep where she sat. "I feel like I've been praying in the back of my mind for hours."

"Me, too."

"Funny. You used to make fun of me for praying." Her head fell into the crook of his neck. Cascades of curls tickled his skin. His lips brushed the top of her head before he could catch himself. Then his shoulders stiffened. What was happening here? Nicky had hardly been willing to let her guard down this way before. Could it be that he had somehow dropped his guard just enough to let her see how much he was still drawn to her? No, he couldn't let them get any closer. Her life and his were in very different places. And he was hardly the kind of man she deserved.

A deep yawn left her lungs and Luke nearly chuckled in relief. For a moment he'd been worried, but she was probably just too exhausted to hold her head up a moment longer. In fact, he knew the feeling. Well, if she needed a friend, she had one in him.

Luke let one hand slide over hers, just long enough to squeeze it. "Yeah, Nicky, I pray now. I have prayed every single day for many, many years. I gave up a lot of the person I used to be when I met George. Mocking people who believed in God was one of the first things I stopped doing."

A faint smile crossed her lips. "How did you even meet George? You've never told me."

He took a deep breath. It was the wrong time to tell her this. But maybe he'd run out of better chances to tell her the truth.

That night she'd been standing alone on the lookout cliff side between Camp Sprit and Ace Sports waiting for a guy who was never going to show, he'd been sitting alone, in a jail cell, facing the future he so fully deserved. *Well, you see, I wasn't just a liar when you knew me, I was also a thief. George caught me stealing the camp's cash box...*

"Well, if this isn't the most depressing campfire I've ever seen!" Bear's voice boomed. Luke didn't think he'd seen Bear smile once since they'd set off that morning, but now Bear's intoxicated grin was wide

enough for ten men or more. "I don't know why everyone's in such a big hurry to get out of this place. This
island is amazing. I say we all get a good night's sleep
and worry about leaving in the morning." He tore off a
mouthful of bread and chewed it with his mouth open.

As much as Luke hated to admit it, it might be the
only option they had left. His own body ached with
fatigue and Nicky was yawning so deeply he half expected her to pass out on the ground. Her eyes had already closed.

Luke lowered his head toward her. "How about it?"
he asked softly. "Why don't we all plan to get some
sleep and head out at first light?"

She shook her head, but her eyes didn't open. "Can't.
Need to leave. There's a hunter."

A flurry of whispers yanked his attention across
the circle. Aaron and Gracie were arguing about something, but he couldn't make out what they were saying.

Another yawn from Nicky. Luke's fingers brushed
under her chin. Her eyes fluttered open. "Nicola?
Sweetheart? You're exhausted. Why don't you go lie
down for fifteen or twenty minutes at least? Have a
nap. I'll wake you if Trevor arrives." Even if they didn't
see Trevor until morning, she was in no position to paddle. "I promise, if Trevor doesn't come back with the
boat, and we all end up having to stay the night while
Bear sleeps his liquor off, I will stay up all night and
keep watch by the fire while you sleep."

Her head bobbed drowsily. "I'll keep watch for you
to sleep, too. We'll do shifts."

A smile crossed his lips. Same old, stubborn, independent Nicky. "Deal."

Aaron and Gracie's argument seemed to be growing. Gracie knocked a bowl of stew from Aaron's hands and bolted into one of the tents. Aaron turned and strode off into the woods. Luke glanced at Nicky. She hadn't even seemed to notice. "Gracie's gone into the tent. Why don't you follow her?" He stretched. "I think it's about time Aaron and I talk."

Not to mention, it probably wasn't the safest idea for Aaron to be running alone and upset through the woods right now. Either Aaron was in danger or he was part of the danger. Regardless, he was going to confront Aaron now, once and for all. And just let him try to squirm out of telling Luke the whole truth this time.

He waited just long enough to watch Nicky stumble into the same tent as Gracie and close the flaps behind her. Then Luke stood. Vertigo swept over him like an ocean. His head swam. He blinked hard. *Must be more tired than I'd realized.* Luke waved in Bear's direction. "I'll be back in a minute."

Then he hurried in the direction he'd just seen Aaron disappear. "Hey, Aaron. Wait up!"

No answer other than the sound of his own body pushing through the trees. Branches smacked his face. The path disappeared under his feet. Luke pressed on. His feet tumbled down the hill, propelled by wobbly legs. "Aaron? Hey? You out here?"

Pain pounded through his head now. The forest melted and shifted around him. Luke stumbled over a log and nearly fell to his knees. He told his legs to move, but they didn't want to listen. Something was wrong with his head. *Something was seriously wrong.* He was having trouble thinking clearly, and his body was so sluggish he could barely stumble.

He wasn't just tired. Or even sick. This felt more like the hazy, disoriented fog that used to collapse into his brain as a teenager when he stole some of his mother's sleeping pills to dull his own pain.

He'd been drugged.

Luke spun around. He had to get back to camp. *He had to warn Nicky.* His feet stumbled. His knees hit the ground and he rolled downhill for a few minutes before he could stop himself. The lake rushed up to meet him. A wall of canoes hovered on the sand to his left. He was on the beach, but he didn't remember heading for the shore.

A shape loomed ahead of him in the darkness. Camouflage fatigues. Green balaclava.

The Hunter.

"Who are you?" Luke struggled to his feet.

The blow was hard, fast and unrelenting as something hard and heavy smashed against his temple.

God! Help me. Help Nicky. Help—

Luke fell forward. His face struck the dirt. Then the world went black.

TWELVE

Nicky opened her eyes. Sunlight filtered through the open tent flap. She blinked. Then she tried to swallow. Her throat ached and her mouth felt as though she'd swallowed cotton balls. She hadn't even kicked her boots off before her body had landed on top of a camp cot. How long had she been asleep? She fumbled for her watch with aching arms that didn't seem to want to move. It was six forty-five.

Somehow she'd slept more than ten hours, if you could even call that sleeping. It had felt more like she'd been floating in and out of consciousness, never quite awake and never quite asleep. Weak limbs pushed her body up to sitting. Her head ached. She'd had terrible nightmares, too; their disjointed afterimages still sloshing around her foggy mind.

Someone had been tearing up the camp...scattering equipment, tossing bags open and knocking over the men's tent... Gracie had been screaming... Bear was bellowing... Someone said something about stealing a boat... She'd known they were about to leave... They

*were all going to leave...without her... Then someone
had been standing over her... The Hunter... Watching
her...laughing... She'd tried to cry out for help but he'd
poured something into her mouth... And unconscious-
ness had pulled her back down again...*

She shuddered. Her body and brain felt as they
had one morning after she'd taken a heavy-duty cold
medication she hadn't realized had a sleep aid in it—
multiplied by a thousand. She pressed her fingers
against her eyes. They stung. Had she been crying in
her sleep?

Gracie was gone, along with her sleeping bag. Nicky
grabbed a bottle of water from her bag and chugged
it as though she hadn't tasted water in days. A gentle
breeze was whispering at the edge of the open tent flap.
The sound of bird song filled her ears. But she couldn't
hear any voices. Nicky forced her sluggish body across
the floor and stumbled through the open flap.

Her hand rose to her lips. What had happened?

The campsite had been trashed. The men's tent lay
on the ground in a pile of broken poles and canvas.
Most of the bags were gone; their contents strewed over
the ground. She stumbled through the wreckage. The
food was missing. The first-aid kit was gone. So were
the tinder box and matches. The water jug had been
tipped over and poured out into the dirt.

Every corner of the camp had been raided as if by
scavengers in a hurry to grab whatever they could and
run. Someone had even snapped off one of the tent
poles. *She'd somehow slept through this?*

Prayers poured through her lips, her pleas for the

safety of the others mingled with questions she couldn't even begin to put into words. Who could have possibly done this? Was it the Hunter? Had nobody tried to stop him? Why had she thought she'd heard Gracie screaming? Where was Gracie? And Aaron? And Bear? And Luke...?

She swallowed hard. *Please Lord, let Luke be all right. Let everyone be all right.*

Her eyes fell across the empty log where they'd piled the wetsuits and life jackets the night before, and the reality of the situation slipped like oil into her gut.

Some of the life jackets were gone. What if everyone really had left and they'd taken the canoes?

Nicky ran through the forest and down the path toward the water, forcing her heavy legs to move until she could feel their strength beginning to return. Finally she could see the crystal-blue water sparkling ahead of her through the breaks in the trees. She stumbled down the hill toward the beach. There was no motorboat tethered to the dock. Trevor still hadn't returned.

Luke was lying, fully clothed, on his back in the water. Her heart stopped.

He couldn't be dead. He just couldn't! She'd just found him again.

A cry slipped through her lips.

He raised his head and his weary eyes met hers with an unshielded, unguarded look that was so full of ferocity, affection and relief it took her breath away.

"Nicky, you're..." His eyes rose to heaven as a rush of emotion made his voice husky. "Thank You, God."

She kicked off her boots and ran to him. Without

thinking. Without question. Without hesitation. Her body splashed into the water, barely feeling the cold and damp sink into her dirty clothes.

He caught her in waist-deep water and pulled her into his arms. Her hands slid around his neck. Tears poured from her eyes. His grip tightened. His lips brushed over her head as he murmured thankful prayers into her hair. Then she titled her face toward him and his mouth found hers.

She kissed him back sweetly, gently, allowing herself to feel the comfort of his lips and the roughness of his cheeks for barely a moment.

What was she doing? She was just scared, hurt and relived he was okay. Not to mention still groggy from whatever she'd been drugged with and shaken by the chaos of whatever had happened in the night. But then, why was he kissing her? The echo of their former connection and the attraction they'd once felt for each other seemed to flow through the air around them. She'd felt it. He obviously had, too. But still, they needed to rise above it.

She loosened her grip. He pulled back. She slid her arms out from around his neck, until they were an arm's-length apart.

Luke blinked. "I'm sorry. I was out of line." He ran two wet hands over his face. "My head's really foggy. But that's no excuse."

She brushed her fingers against his temple. "You're bleeding."

He touched his head. "It's not as bad as it looks. Someone knocked me out. The Hunter, I think. But I was drugged with a pretty heavy dose of something before that, so who knows what I actually saw. I only woke up on the beach a few moments ago, too sluggish and thirsty to move. So I crawled into the lake to wake up." His fingers brushed her hair. "But how are you? Are you hurt? Did anyone…?" The words froze on his tongue.

"Hurt me?" She shook her head. "No. But they drugged me. I think it was in the stew. I got all woozy and out of it, then passed out and had terrible nightmares. At one point I thought the Hunter was in my tent, standing there, watching me sleep, and that he then poured more drugs down my throat to make sure I stayed asleep. But it's all very foggy.

"When I woke up, the campsite was trashed, everything was ransacked and everyone else was gone. I thought for a moment that everyone had just taken the canoes and gone back to the mainland without me."

"They didn't take the canoes. They couldn't have." Luke turned her face toward the shore.

The canoes all lay on the beach. Someone had smashed them to pieces.

Luke half expected Nicky to collapse into his arms again. But instead she rolled her shoulders back and started for the shore.

"I honestly thought for a moment that everyone had left without me." She was repeating herself, and something about it irritated him.

"Well, that's probably just a side effect of whatever we were drugged with." He followed her to shore. "You must have known there was no way I would just leave the island without you."

She turned. An eerie calm spread down her face, wiping away any trace of the vulnerable woman he'd been comforting just moments before. "Wouldn't you? I mean, not maliciously. Not in a mean way. But, if you thought it was the best thing under the circumstances—"

He couldn't believe what he was hearing. "No! Of course I wouldn't!" His voice echoed through the empty beach, only a couple of notches less than yelling. "How could you possibly think I would ever go anywhere without you knowing that you were in danger?"

Nicky picked her boots up off the beach and pulled them on swiftly, balancing on one foot as she did so. Then she wrung the water from her hair and tied it into a bun with an elastic she pulled from her pocket. One moment she'd been tumbling into his arms with the same youthful abandon she used to all those years ago. Now she looked ready to take on the world, singlehandedly.

"I'm sorry. I didn't mean to offend you. Obviously something happened to the others, and they're gone." Nicky strode down the beach. Red fiberglass splinters crunched beneath her feet. "Hopefully one of these canoes isn't too badly damaged and we can patch it up with a piece of tarp and duct tape."

She stopped by the first canoe. It looked as though someone had taken a sledgehammer to it. Her tongue clicked over her teeth. "Ideally, if we get one of them seaworthy, you can paddle to shore for help."

It was as if she was determined to ignore the fact he'd just said he wasn't about to leave her. He didn't know if it was because she wanted him to go or if she was just trying to prepare herself for what she thought he was going to do anyway. Would be nice if she had a bit more faith in him. He flipped over the second canoe. It had been hit so hard it had practically split down the middle. "And, hypothetically, where will you be while I'm paddling to shore in a patchwork canoe?"

She picked up pieces of a broken paddle. Someone had snapped it in two. Nothing they'd seen so far looked salvageable. "The campers are obviously still on the island somewhere, and I'm going to try to find them. Hopefully, Trevor just reverted back to his lazy, slow-moving self last night and is going to come boating back to us as soon as he wakes up this morning. George would never let him leave us like this."

Luke shook his head as though there was water in his ears. "You want me to paddle for help, while you stay here alone?"

"Yes, while I search the island for Aaron, Gracie and Bear." She sucked in a breath. "Oh, and Russ, too. He must still be on the island, because all the canoes are accounted for." She moved on to the third canoe.

"Nicky. Stop. Listen, I am going nowhere— nowhere—without you. I know this isn't the situation either of us would have chosen, but I'm the guy God's apparently dropped here to help you get through this alive. So, whatever happens next, you and I are in this thing together. I am not going anywhere without you. Trust me on this."

She ran her hand all the way down her arm from shoulder to wrist, as the professional mask slipped from her eyes just enough to let him see the mixture of fear and courage brewing inside.

"I'm sorry if I gave you the wrong impression. I never should have kissed you like that. Maybe this isn't fair of me—and maybe the sleeping pills in my system and the fear of the past couple of days are hitting me harder than I realized—but whenever you say stuff like that I'm always going to remember that you're that same guy who looked in my eyes and promised me all kinds of things and then left without even saying goodbye."

He felt the words drop into his gut like stones. "That's different."

She turned her back to him and started for the next canoe. "I know. But sometimes it feels exactly the same."

"Trust me, it's totally different. That time, I was in jail!" He crossed the space between them in two strides. His hand brushed her shoulder. "Remember how I told you I was a runaway? Not to mention an all-around lousy person? Well, that night I broke into the lodge and stole the camp cash box. *That's* how I met George. He caught me stealing, dragged my sorry hide off to the police, then came back to bail me out the next morning. And I've done everything in my power to pay him back for that mercy."

She still hadn't turned. Her arm was rigid under his touch.

He sighed. "Come on, Nicola. Can't you see it's a

good thing I didn't come back after that? You deserved so much better in your life than a guy like me. The healthier I got and the more I grew up, the clearer and clearer that became to me."

She turned slowly. The color had drained from her face. She tried to speak, but the sounds choked in her throat. She stumbled forward and suddenly Luke could see the blood-stained sand spreading out beneath her feet. There was a body lying on its back, eyes staring unseeingly at the skies above. One rigid hand grasped the deadly arrow embedded deep inside his chest.

It was Russ Tusk.

THIRTEEN

They covered Russ's body the best they could, burying him in chunks of broken canoes like a funeral mound. Then Luke dropped to his knees in silent prayer beside the body. Anger burned in his chest. A man was dead. Shot down like an animal for what? Because of the evil in another man's heart? Had Russ been in league with the Hunter? Or had he just been in the wrong place at the wrong time? Either way, he didn't deserve for his life to end this way. *God, have mercy. Please bring this man's killer to justice. Don't let another person be hurt by his cruelty.* Nicky knelt beside him for a moment. Tears trickled lightly down her cheek, and everything inside his chest ached to wipe them away. "We need a plan for getting off this island."

She nodded, then stood and wiped the dirt from her jeans. "No amount of duct tape is going to make one of these seaworthy. And you're right, we're probably safer sticking together. Until right now, I thought the Hunter was only out to sabotage things and wasn't actually trying to kill anyone. I was obviously wrong.

Our best option now is to scavenge what we can from the camp and the obstacle course to build a raft. If we can find the others while we're at it, all the better."

They turned and walked back up the path toward the camp. "Also, I'm still not giving up hope that Trevor decided yesterday that taking a couple of people to hospital was a reasonable excuse to take the evening off, and he's going to eventually get back here with that motorboat."

"Do you trust him?"

"Trevor? Nope. Not as far as I could throw him. But I trust George." She cast him a dry, sideways glance. "Sounds like you do, too."

In the aftermath of finding Russ's body, they hadn't paused a moment to talk about Luke's confession about the stolen camp cash box or ending up in a jail cell. Maybe there wasn't much to say.

"We should also search the island for the Hunter's boat," he said. "He must have some kind of watercraft moored here somewhere."

"Agreed. I just can't imagine where."

They kept walking. With every breath that filled his chest, Luke could feel the desire inside him to protect the wild, tenacious beauty walking beside him. Nicky deserved a life—a life every bit as wonderful as she was, filled with all her ambitious, creative dreams coming true.

Lord, You know I'd do whatever it takes to make that happen. But how can I protect her when I can't even see the danger?

For a moment he almost wished he hadn't left his

own handmade bow back in the car. Not that a six-foot-tall wooden bow was the right weapon to go stalking through the woods with, or that any of the purely recreational arrows in his quiver would've been good against a human target.

The trees parted and the campsite came into view. Wow. She wasn't kidding. The place was such a mess it looked as though a herd of wild animals had gone trampling through it. They started scouring the ground, working without talking, turning over every package and piece of equipment they could find.

"So what would you have done with this place?" Nicky bent to pick up the remains of her bag.

"You mean the island?"

"Yeah." She dumped the contents out on the ground. A pair of jeans and two T-shirts tumbled out. She frowned and stuffed them back in the bag. "Because of location and logistics, we've only really used the island for staff training and a few off-season camps. But like I said yesterday, George's dream was to turn this into a place for the kinds of teens who are either in trouble with the law or at risk of going that way."

The ones like *him* in other words. "This would actually be a good place for a camp like that," he said. "No cell phone service means no quick phone calls to your drug dealer. There's nowhere to run away to and nothing to steal."

She started picking through the broken tent. "Obviously if the Hunter scares future campers and donors away, this camp is dead in the water. Unless God gives me a sudden fortune to buy this place from George myself, which somehow I don't see happening. But, say I do still get to dream, the top things on my list for the island are to improve the beach, make the caves safe for spelunking and clear the water under that big rock so people can dive off it safely. So, as a former petty thug turned sports reporter, what kind of activities would you run?"

He grinned. That was one way of putting it. "I like archery a lot actually. Not the fancy tech like the Hunter's using. But the old-fashioned, wooden bows back at camp, where you really feel the draw and need to focus all your energy on making the shot. It's a lot harder to hit the target, but it teaches discipline and consistency."

"Okay. How about paint ball? Too violent?"

"No, not at all. It teaches kids teamwork and focus, not to mention is a healthy outlet for aggression." A muddy box of granola bars crunched under his feet. He picked it up. Two bars left. He tossed them both to Nicky. "Obviously you're also thinking obstacle courses."

She caught both bars in one hand. Then she tossed one of them right back to him. "Obviously."

"You should also really look into combining a large-scale, ground-based obstacle course with a run through the woods. I've done a few runs for charity with the team at *Torchlight News*." Won all them, too. Nobody knew how to duck and run the way he did.

Her smile was hesitant, as if debating whether or not to let the words she was thinking pass her lips. "If we do manage to stay on our feet a bit longer, would you be willing to come up and help show us how to run one?"

He let out a long breath. "Actually, George has invited me up to volunteer in the past. But I've told him it's not really my thing. I'd be happy to email you a few links to web sites, though."

"Right. I'd forgotten. You're not a 'kids and families' kind of guy."

What did she mean by that? Yes, he'd said that. But not because he didn't care. He cared a lot. "Knowing you're no good at something isn't the same as not caring about it. Look, I love kids and would have loved to have had my own, and I'll do everything I can to support this camp, too. I just didn't think the guy who tried to steal the camp cash box should be anyone's first choice to teach campers anything." He'd never forget the sight of the metal box sitting on a table in the police station as George counted out dollars and quarters to help Luke make bail. Nicky turned around and he could see words flashing in her eyes ready to fly out her mouth at him. But he wasn't in the mood to argue about this.

"Look, yes, I'm great at all kinds of sports stuff— shooting, running, dodging, diving—but you want to know what I'm best at? Not the whole extroverted, leading people and team motivation stuff you do. My strength is tactics and strategy. I'm the guy standing in the locker room with a blue marker and big whiteboard figuring out who goes where—"

Luke froze as he heard words leave his mouth with the clarity of a starting whistle. Here he'd been so busy telling God that he was the wrong man to have Nicky's back because he didn't know how to solve crime, he forgot to remember what kind of man he was. He was the kind of man who understood how games were played.

Focus, Luke. The Hunter is treating you and Nicky like prey. Hunting you. Sabotaging you. Trapping you here. Think like an opponent. So, what kind of game is the Hunter playing?

Suddenly he could feel the events of the past few days spread out in front of his mind's eye like figures on a whiteboard. "In the end, it's all about knowing your opponent."

"You've lost me." Nicky's eyes were on his face.

Something crackled in the woods like the sound of falling branches. He scanned the trees. One hand reached for hers. The other rose to his lips. He led her toward the one tent still left standing, thankful she was willing to follow without question. They stepped inside and pulled the flaps closed behind them. Then he leaned toward her, barely letting his voice rise above a whisper. He was tired of being watched. It was about time they had a team meeting without worrying someone might be listening in.

"When you build obstacle courses you probably spend ages plotting out how every single hook, notch and board fits together to take someone from the start to the finish. Right?"

She nodded. "Of course."

"So, let's do the same thing with the whole 'hunter' thing. Where is he going with all this? See, I don't know about you, but I'm tired of feeling like we're just swept up in a series of random attacks, as if we were battling nothing but a mindless animal. When in actual fact, we're fighting a man who probably wants something specific and is doing what he thinks he needs to do to get it."

Understanding dawned in her hazel eyes. "His end game."

"Right."

He sat on the bare-board floor. She sat opposite him. "I've been busy looking at everyone around us as suspects. Aaron's been acting suspicious. He gets in a fight with Russ, then Russ turns up dead. Something's off with Gracie, too. I just can't put my finger on what. Trevor didn't come back with the boat, which could mean something bad has happened. Bear has a history of threatening people. It's clear you never trusted Neil of Ace Sports.

"I can find reasons to suspect anyone of anything. Which gets us nowhere. When what I really need to be doing is looking at the Hunter himself." He sighed heavily as he shoved his fingers through his hair. "Am I making any sense at all?"

She nodded. "Crystal clear. You're saying we need to stop scanning the bushes for every little snap and rustle of movement, and instead we need to look at what the Hunter is *aiming* at. Because once we know his target, we'll know who he is."

Yes! Exactly that! He could have almost kissed her. Nicky had always been so very good at helping him sort his thoughts when his brain was spinning. His grin grew wide. "You've got it. So, what was his first target?"

"The lodge."

"Why the lodge?"

Her answer came automatically. "Because basically the lodge is the heart of Camp Spirit. It's where we cook meals, feed campers, lead Sunday chapel services, have arts and crafts… Not to mention it's where we kept all our camp records and computers. He went straight for our heart and took out the camp's brain in the process."

"The camp's 'brain'?"

A slight smile crossed her lips. "George. He's the brains of this operation."

He nodded. Yes, the fire had taken out George and delayed them finding out whatever plans had been going on in that brain of his. "Do you think someone was trying to kill you and George?"

Her head shook. "Considering George's age and health, there are lots and lots of easier ways to kill him and make it look like an accident. A fire that large takes planning, not to mention the sprinkler system and fire alarm were disabled. The Hunter had no way of knowing we'd be there, let alone that I'd be in the loft and unable to get George out safely. So, no, I don't think he was trying to kill us. Then his second attack only reinforces that. The Hunter jumped me on the island but let me go without a scrape."

"He hardly just let you go. He shoved your face into the ground and held a knife to your neck."

"But he could have cut me or killed me, and he didn't. He just ran away and stole the boat."

He ran his hand over his chin. "True."

"Then, he vandalized the obstacle course, apparently drugged our stew somehow and then destroyed the canoes." Nicky ticked the items off on her fingers. "Every step of the way it's like he was trying to scare us and sabotage this camp. But not intentionally kill anyone. In fact, if Russ hadn't been murdered I'd have thought his end goal was just to anger the sponsors and dissuade them from helping us."

A howl of fury shook the air outside the tent followed by a crash that sounded like metal pots being hurled against rocks. A voice swore loudly like the cry of a wounded animal. Luke leaped to his feet, shielding Nicky with his body. The canvas was torn back and they found themselves staring into the cold, metal barrel of Bear's handgun.

"Get me off this island. Now!" Bear waved his weapon in Nicky's face. "Or I will blow both your heads off."

Looked like alcohol wasn't the only thing the Bear had managed to conceal on his person and smuggle onto the island. She scrambled to her feet, feeling her heart pounding in her chest. "We aren't the ones who destroyed the canoes. Trust me, we want to get off the island as much as you do."

"Trust you?" Bear's laugh turned into a roar. Bloodshot eyes bulged. "I don't know what kind of sick, twisted scheme you think you're running here. But I came out here on this camping trip in good faith because rumor had it your boss was about to pull something big and I thought it might be good for business. First you ask me to climb on some obstacle thing that nearly kills someone. Then you *drug* me.

"Next thing I know, I think I'm hearing trees running around, watching a tent fly and getting trapped in a battle with who knows what, until I wake up lying in a stream."

It sounded as though the drugs had hit Bear even harder than her and Luke. Then again, he'd gulped that stew down by the bowlful. Bear had probably consumed more than half the pot, not to mention he'd been drunk. It was no wonder he'd been hallucinating.

"I didn't come here to be chased through the woods like some kind of wild animal while someone shot arrows at my back."

"Someone shot arrows at you?" Luke asked. "Are you sure? Did you see what they looked like?"

Bear snorted. "Oh, like you don't know. It was little woodland fairies." The gun waved closer to Luke. "Now, come on. Out of the tent. We're going to take a walk." His eyes narrowed. "And don't even think of trying anything or I'll shoot."

Nicky watched as Luke stepped out of the tent, careful to keep his body positioned between her and the weapon. He was protecting her. Her heart ached for him. For so very long the memory of this man had made her feel alone and rejected. Now, here he was, in the flesh, and for the first time in her whole life, making her feel *protected*.

She prayed. *Please, Lord. Don't let him be hurt on account of me. Keep him safe. Show him—show me—what to do.*

"Where are we going?" Luke's voice was firm and steady.

Bear gestured wildly toward the trees. "We're going to get your boat. Then we're going to get into that boat and you're going to take me off this island and back to the mainland."

Nicky followed Luke out of the tent and stood just behind his shoulder. "I'm sorry, Bear. The canoes are smashed—"

"I don't care about the canoes! I want you to take me to the motorboat!"

She shook her head. "Trevor hasn't come back with the motorboat yet—"

"Of course he has! Don't you dare lie to me!"

What? Nicky's jaw dropped. What on earth was he talking about? If Trevor had returned, the only place he'd have moored was at the dock, and he'd have hardly left again without her. Had Bear been so drugged on sleeping pills that he'd hallucinated seeing an actual motorboat? Or had he actually stumbled on where the Hunter had hidden his? She took a step forward and shot a sideways glance at Luke.

But Luke's eyes were focused on Bear. "Have you seen the boat since you woke up this morning?"

Bear rolled his eyes. "I don't have time for this." Before Nicky could react, he reached out and grabbed her by the shoulder. "Nicky is going to get me down to that boat."

His grip was so tight it made her eyes water. Beside her, she could see every muscle in Luke's body tense, as though he was waiting for his moment to strike.

"You have to know that I'm not about to let you hurt her."

Bear chuckled. "You honestly think you can stop me?"

She did. Suddenly, with every fiber of her being, she knew that Luke would either save her or die trying. How wrong she'd been. All this time she thought he'd never really cared about her, beyond some superficial desire to kiss a lonely girl. Now, here he was, standing beside her, willing to take a bullet to keep her safe. Did he have any idea that she'd do the same for him?

Please, give me wisdom, Lord. Please help us find a way out of this where no one gets hurt. Especially if Bear really has seen a boat that could get us all out of here.

Nicky gritted her teeth against the pain and raised her chin to look Bear straight in the eye. "There's no need to threaten me, Bear. If you show me where the boat is, I'm happy to get everyone off this island. And I'm guessing Luke would agree with me on that."

A silence spread through the wrecked campsite, punctuated only by the rustle of tree branches. She watched as Luke's clear blue-gray eyes searched over every inch of her face, then turned to the heavens above, before finally fixing their hard stare on the man now holding a gun to her face.

"We're not your enemy. We have no clue who drugged us, or trashed the camp, or was shooting arrows at you. Let go of Nicky, now, and we will all go see the boat you found together."

"Save your breath. I'm not about to trust you, and you're in no place to negotiate." Bear's fat hand grabbed a fistful of her hair. "Oh, and I'm definitely going to take her to that boat—"

Luke stepped toward him. His grin had teeth and more than a little bite.

"Let me guess. You ran out of alcohol last night and woke with a hangover so bad you think the island is spinning and your skull's about to split open. Well, just because you can wave your gun around doesn't mean for one moment you're steady enough to hit your target. Now maybe you'll be stupid and fire that gun, anyway—and you might hurt Nicky, or you might hurt me, or you might put a bullet through your own toe. Either way, you'll be no closer to getting off this island. You obviously can't get to the boat without us, or you'd have done it already. So, I'll say it again—take your hands off her."

Bear tried laughing again but the sound echoed hollow in his throat. He shrugged and let go. "Fine. But my gun stays pointed at her head and you stay back. I don't actually want to hurt her, but like you said, my aim's a little shaky right now." He snickered. "And seeing the way you look at her, I don't think you're about to take that chance."

They walked. While Bear had let go of her body, his fingers still poked her just below the shoulder blade, as if to steer her. He needn't have bothered. She could tell exactly where they were headed—to the giant diving rock where she and Luke had stood and watched the Hunter peel off in her boat two nights before.

It was the last place anyone would stash a boat. The huge rock mass jutted out into the lake like a great big boulder, maybe two stories above the water's surface. As David had pointed out yesterday, the spot was perfect for diving, or at least it would be when they cleared some of the more dangerous rocks out of the water below. But there was absolutely nowhere there to moor a boat.

They stepped out of the limited protection of the forest cover and onto the bare and empty rock. Bright sunlight bounced off the crystal waters. The lake spread out below them, calm and empty, all the way to the distant shores beyond. There wasn't a single boat in sight.

Bear walked her right to the edge. "Found it hours ago then spent all morning trying to figure out how to get down there to it."

"Down where?" But the words had barely left her lips before she heard the unmistakable knocking sound of an aluminum boat rocking against the shore. She stepped to the edge of the cliff and looked down. A Camp Spirit motorboat was floating, empty, up against the bottom of diving rock. A gasp escaped her lips. How on earth had it gotten there? And why was it empty?

Even from here she could tell the motor was twisted at a funny angle. The blades had no doubt been broken off and damaged by impact, and even from a distance she could see the outline of liquid pooling in the bottom. It was either water from a hull leak or gasoline from a hole in the tank. While the boat might be the best way off the island they'd found yet, it was hardly ready to just be fired up to hit the open water, even if it had been easy to get to.

She turned back. Bear was standing so close he was nearly nudging her toes over the edge. But she fixed her gaze on Luke. He was several paces back but slowly closing the gap between them.

"Bear's right, Luke," she called. "There is a Camp Spirit motorboat down there. I can't actually tell if it's the one the Hunter stole or the one that Trevor and the other campers left in yesterday. Either way, it's pretty badly damaged."

Bear leaned toward her until his sweaty red face was barely inches from hers. "So take me down there!"

"There isn't a path down there." She gritted her teeth. "I'd have to try to either jump down and miss hitting it somehow or swim around the island to it. Even then, I doubt we'll be able to get the motor to work."

Pebbles shifted beneath her feet. Luke inched closer. She had to focus on keeping Bear's attention long enough to give Luke a chance to knock the gun from his hand. If only they weren't standing so close to the edge, she'd risk kicking Bear's legs out from under him. But either one could knock him off the rock and into the water—maybe even taking her with him—and after her last attempted dive off this rock she knew you had to leap out pretty far if you wanted to safely clear the rocks below.

Another snort from Bear. The gun pressed up against her cheek. "I don't believe you."

"I don't care whether or not you do." Her voice rose louder. "I'm telling the truth. Honestly, the best thing right now would be if you let Luke and me figure out a way to get down there. Maybe if we repair a couple of paddles, we can all paddle it together to the mainland. But we can't help you as long as you're being threatening and irrational. So…please. Stop, drop the gun and let us save you."

Cold, icy black swept through Bear's eyes. He flicked the safety off his gun. "How about I just shoot you instead?"

An arrow flew from the woods. It sizzled as it arched high above them. Then fell toward the boat below. An explosion shook the water. Smoke and flame engulfed the tiny vessel. The motorboat was on fire.

FOURTEEN

Luke watched as a masked figure in green hunting fatigues stepped slowly out of the woods. With one steady hand, the Hunter gripped a high-tech bow. With the other he aimed an arrow straight at Luke's heart.

Instinctively, Luke's hands rose in a fighter's stance. In front of him stood a deadly killer and the camp's saboteur. Behind his back, Bear still had Nicky tight in his grip, a gun to her head. Below them, the motorboat burned.

Luke's eyes looked to the sky. *Well, Lord, it looks like I'm finally stuck with nowhere left to run. Whatever it takes, help me get Nicky out of this alive. Whatever happens next, thank You for giving me a chance to try to make things right with her.*

The Hunter's string drew back. Luke set his jaw and glanced at the strong, wild, beautiful woman he'd shield from danger even if it ended up costing his life. Her lips moved as she mouthed one single word. *"Jump."*

Nicky drove the heel of her palm down into the bridge of Bear's nose. With a roar, Bear loosened his grip just enough to let Nicky kick back hard against the rock. She dove, backward, her body cutting through the air even as an arrow flew into the empty space where she'd been standing.

Luke turned and ran after her, expecting with every breath to feel the fatal blow of a bullet between his eyes or an arrow to his back. For a second it was as if the world moved in slow motion. Bear's gun went off. The bullet ricocheted off the rocks. The bow twanged. Bear fell to the ground, an arrow deep in his chest. Luke leaped. Arrow feathers ruffled his hair. Smoke and fire rushed toward him. He closed his eyes as burning air filled his lungs.

He hit the water and felt his body go under. He opened his eyes, disoriented to see nothing but darkness on all sides and the flicker of the fire's reflection. Instinctively he kicked and his leg smacked against a rock. Then he felt a hand brush his shoulder. He grabbed it and let it guide him to the surface.

Luke broke through the surface beside Nicky. The charred remains of the motorboat burned like a bonfire in front of him. Flames danced on the surface of the water. Heat flickered through the air like a haze. The stench of burning gasoline filled the air. He glanced up and saw nothing but a blanket of smoke. Well, at least that should shield them from the Hunter's sights.

"You okay?" Nicky treaded water behind him. Her face was pale. Soot clung to the edges of her long, dark hair. But her eyes danced with a light that brought fresh air to his lungs.

"Alive and kicking." They swam to the rocks just

under the rock face. Then she hugged him, deeply, clutching him to her chest and tangling her limbs through his, like a life jacket. His hand ran through her hair. His lip brushed her cheek. She turned toward him, her mouth just inches from his.

Every beat of his heart was telling him to take her firmly and kiss her like a man. *But what kind of man? A man like his father? A man who'd hurt women? A man not fit to be a husband or father? Could he really expect the blood burning through his veins was what any woman would choose for the father of her children?*

Smoke stung his eyes. He closed them tightly. "I think Bear is dead. The Hunter shot him right in the chest."

Her face paled to the color of ash. She slipped her arms from his body. "I'm sorry. I was just so relieved when I realized you were alive, that for a second I didn't even process anything else except…"

The fact I was alive? Yeah. I felt the exact same way about you.

"It's okay. As I'm sure you know, when something bad happens, it normally takes our brains a couple of ticks until it starts thinking like it should. Bear shot at the Hunter and missed. The Hunter finished him off before he could fire again."

Her eyes ran over the boat's burning hull. "He also effectively just destroyed our best chance to get off this island. I can't salvage anything from it now. Not a flotation device, a radio, a paddle…none of it." She sighed. "Whatever kind of incendiary arrow he used to set this boat on fire, he knew exactly what he was doing. Judging by the stench, the boat was drenched in gasoline even before the arrow hit it."

"Is that the same boat the Hunter stole two nights ago? Or the one Trevor took the others to shore in yesterday?"

She squinted into the smoke. "I don't know. It's too damaged to tell. But I'm hoping it's the same one he took, otherwise that means Trevor, and maybe even David, Theresa and Martin are in serious danger. But it's clear he planned to scuttle the boat."

The Hunter had to have known that Bear had found the boat hours ago. He could have destroyed it at any time. Instead, he'd waited until Nicky had found the boat, let her see it, get her hopes up and then destroyed it in front of her. Just as she'd been there when the obstacle course had fallen and the lodge had burned. He might have even stood there and watched her sleep. It was as if the Hunter was toying with her and terrorizing her more than anyone else. Did Nicky serve some kind of purpose in the Hunter's twisted endgame? And when that moment came, would they be able to stop him?

They half climbed and half swam over the rugged coastline for what felt like more than an hour. Nicky didn't know for sure. She'd somehow lost her watch in the night, and Luke's phone had been destroyed in the fall. But the sun darting in and out between the clouds high above her head told her it was nearing noon. While her stomach told her the granola bars they'd scavenged at the campsite were long gone.

They moved away from the familiar spaces of the cove and beach, out around the wilder, rockier shore. Uneven layers of slippery rock hid in the murky waters. Long seaweed grew four or five feet tall around them. The water was both too shallow to swim and too mucky to walk. But, if the Hunter was looking for them, the beach and cove were probably the first places he'd look, and if he did have a watercraft hidden somewhere on the island, searching the untamed shore would be their best chance to find it.

Her hands grasped a birch sapling growing vertically by the water's edge. She pulled herself to shore and climbed onto a thin ledge of rock. Not much of a seat, but it would do long enough to give her aching body a bit of a break while she caught her breath.

Luke gripped the tree with both hands and hung there for a moment.

"You want to sit?" she said. "I could slide over."

"Nah. I'm good." He smiled *that* one perfect smile that had haunted her dreams for years. That sweet, tender but wry, half grin curling up at just one side of a mouth so rough and yet unbelievably gentle at the same time. She'd always loved it. Maybe it was because there'd always been a lot of huge, wide and toothy overblown smiles in the camping world, from the kind of men who just plastered them on whether they meant them or not. Not to mention those that came from the kind of men who smiled only with their mouths while scowling with their eyes.

But Luke's smile had always been special. It was a rare, genuine, even reluctant smile that somehow spread joy all the way up his cheekbones and crinkled the corners of his eyes. It was a smile that had never seemed forced or fake—

Hang on, and yet it had *been fake! Hadn't it?*

Instinctively she sat straighter and rolled her shoulders back. Her body slipped from the ledge and tumbled into the water. Luke kept hold of the branch with one hand and caught her with the other. His arm wrapped around her waist, pulling her back in. "Are you okay?"

No. Of course she wasn't. She'd been tossed into a life-or-death battle together with the one man who'd once stolen her heart and who even now seemed capable of stealing it from her again. Even though he'd lied to her and left her. Even though he had no intention of ever sharing a life with her.

"What's wrong?" His voice was soft. "Something's bothering you."

She turned her face to the rocky shore as sudden tears filled her eyes. It wasn't fair. She felt transparent around him. His eyes seemed able to read her every thought and mood, while he was still barely more than a stranger to her. Part of her even wanted to yell at him now. Yell at him for stealing and breaking her heart. Yell at him for gently pulling that same damaged heart out of her grasp now, whether he even knew he was doing it or not, and making it beat again.

She bit her lip. *Lord, help me be stronger than this.* She was only hurting herself by even letting her mind think of him that way. Regardless of what had happened when he was a selfish runaway, he wasn't that boy now. Now he was a man she'd grown to trust, respect, admire and believe in. This time, he'd been honest enough not to lead her on. He'd told her plainly that he wasn't going to stay, even if she had wanted to ask him to. And she'd told him she was never going to leave.

"Talk to me, Nicky, please." Luke's fingers brushed her shoulder blades. "Look, I can tell you're upset about something. I know we're stuck and I know it's scary, but we're going to get through this together."

Only there is no "together." She ran her wet fingers over her eyes. "I'm sorry. I was just thinking about what's going to happen when we eventually go back to our normal lives. I'm guessing you're looking forward to getting back to the big city—"

"Hang on." He pressed a finger to her lips. "Listen!"

There was the sound of a motor to their right. It was small and purred like a cat. It sounded too small to be a rescue boat and too far away from the mainland to be a tourist passing by. She nodded to Luke. They sank underwater, with their backs to the rocky shore, until just their eyes were above the water.

A sleek, black, personal watercraft slid into view, looking like a snowmobile on the water or a motorcycle on water skis. The Hunter sat astride its back like an archer on his steed. One hand gripped a titanium hunting bow. His masked face turned toward their hiding place as his gaze scanned the shore. The Hunter paused.

Nicky gasped a breath and ducked underwater. Her lungs burned with the urge to breathe. Luke's hand clenched hers tightly. She waited until the ache for air in her lungs was so desperate she couldn't stand it any longer and then slowly raised her head and gulped for air. The Hunter was gone.

Luke surfaced beside her. "Well, now we know what kind of watercraft he's got."

She nodded. No wonder the Hunter had been able to dart around the rocky shore. A personal watercraft like that was so nimble and sleek it could weave and dodge around obstacles at truly incredible speeds. Just like the fancy titanium bow, the Jet Ski was a pretty impressive and expensive toy. Ace Sports owned several.

"It's not good news, though." She shook her head. "We're in more danger than I realized. If he'd been in something like a kayak or canoe he wouldn't be able to paddle and shoot at the same time, not to mention his speed would be limited. But we'd be sitting ducks against a man on a machine like that. We could have a huge head start and he could still catch up and get ahead of us, shooting at us while he did.

"Which, sadly, makes it even less likely that the four who left yesterday are safe. Between his high-tech bow and his high-tech watercraft, he could have taken out the motorboat either on its way to shore or back." Her heart sank, wondering just how many more victims were out there waiting to be found.

Luke's face was grim. "So, we keep searching the shoreline until we figure out where he keeps it hidden and then we take it from him."

A weary smile crossed her lips. "I like how you think."

They kept half swimming, half crawling around the

shoreline, searching every inlet for a sign of the Hunter's hideaway and straining their ears for the sound of the motor. She tried to keep track of the time by tracing the arc of the sun in the sky. The middle of the day came and went. The sun started its slow decent into the afternoon. Her drenched clothes were a wash of muddy gray. Her limbs ached until her cold, wet body threatened to stop moving. But every time she felt ready to curl up and admit defeat, she could feel the brush of Luke's hand on her shoulder or feel the warmth of his gaze on her face.

They rounded a jagged inlet. Harsh stones stung her hands and banged painfully against her knees. Then she saw a burst of dark and light green on the shoreline that was suspiciously a shade off its surroundings. "I think we just found something."

Beneath a camouflaged hunting tarp and a mass of tangled branches, a narrow cave opening gaped in the rock.

They slipped inside, swam inside a few feet, then slid up onto the welcoming ground of the cave floor and lay there panting a moment. She pulled herself to her feet.

"Wow. I had no idea this was here." Or how the Hunter might have found it. Her eyes searched the thin tunnel disappearing into the darkness. "My guess is that this is where the caves in the middle of the island reach the shore."

Luke stood cautiously. "You're saying that if we follow this tunnel it will take us all the way to the middle of the island?"

"It might. I don't know. But if so, it'll be a really

steep uphill climb on our hands and knees. Not to mention we'll run the risk of getting stuck." She was in no hurry to risk getting trapped somewhere dark, cold and underground.

The remains of a campfire lay at their feet. The coals were cool, but the ground around it was littered with empty water bottles and Camp Spirit food containers.

"Someone's been here recently," Luke said.

Nicky opened one of the containers and tapped a few remaining ounces of granola and dried apple into her palm. "I packed these yesterday. Looks like whoever ransacked the camp brought their spoils here. Let's hope our thief stashed the rest of the food and supplies around here, too."

He nodded. "I'm thinking this is where we make our last stand. The Hunter has got to come back here eventually. When he does, we'll be ready. How about you go investigate a little deeper in to see what food and supplies you can find. I'll stay here and guard the doorway in case he comes back."

"Okay." She took a deep breath, focusing her gaze on the darkness. Then she stepped into the gloom. She'd never been comfortable in dark, tight spaces. But somehow being the one left standing guard at the cave's mouth didn't feel all that much safer. If only Luke was walking with her.

The sounds of dripping water and her own panting breath echoed off the walls. Something crunched under her feet. She bent. It was a plastic water bottle, still sealed shut. She unscrewed the cap and took a drink. Then she stepped in farther, feeling with her hands and feet. A tarp. A bag. A sleeping bag. A broken tent pole. A box of cereal and some cans. *Thank You, God!*

She stood. "Hey, Luke! Good news! We've got food, water, rations and—" The words froze on her tongue as she felt the tip of a knife blade press into the back of her neck.

"Nicky?" Luke's voice floated from the front of the cave. "Everything okay?"

The knife pressed deeper into her skin. A hand clenched her jaw. Then a voice snarled in her ear, "Call back, tell him everything is okay, or I'll kill you."

What, risk them both getting killed that way? No, she wasn't about to sacrifice Luke's safety just because someone with a blade told her to.

She filled her lungs with air and screamed at the top of her lungs. "Run, Luke! Run!"

FIFTEEN

Nicky's screams echoed through the cave. Luke grabbed a heavy rock off the cave floor. His fingers tensed around it. No way he was going to bail on Nicky and leave her there in danger. He ran toward the back of the cave, his head down in a football stance. A bright light flashed across his eyes. A flashlight beam bounced around the walls, filling his vision with dazzling spots of light. His arm rose to strike—

"Luke, stop. It's okay." Nicky's voice was strained but strong. "It's okay. We're not going to hurt you. Just let me go. Nobody needs to get hurt."

He froze. Who was she talking to? Then the beam of light fell to the cave floor and Luke traced it back to Gracie's pale, terrified face.

"Drop the rock." Gracie's voice trembled. The flashlight shook in her hands.

"I can't do that. Not until I see Nicky and know she's safe."

Gracie swung the light deeper into the cave and shapes swam into view. A pile of food and supplies was stacked against the cave wall. Nicky was down on her knees. Her hands were raised behind her head, but her face was calm. Luke tensed to spring. Then the shadows shifted and Luke saw the pale, determined face of the young man now holding knife to her throat.

It was Aaron.

"Don't worry, Aaron's going to let me go," Nicky said firmly. Her tone of voice was so strong it could have sliced through brick. "Trust me. Aaron and Gracie must know we're not their enemies and we're just here to help them get off the island."

Did they know that? How could she be sure Aaron and Gracie weren't the ones they should be running from? Luke glanced at Gracie. She'd set the flashlight down at her feet, where it now sent a pale light cascading over the scene.

"Or I could simply take Gracie hostage unless you let Nicky go." Luke was being rhetorical, but he watched sheer panic fill Aaron's eyes. Yeah, there was no way Aaron would ever risk anything happening to Gracie.

But even as the words crossed his lips, Nicky shook her head. "No, Luke. We're not going to do anything to Gracie or use her as leverage. Because Aaron knows Gracie needs our help, and that we're only here to help her." Nicky's eyes burned with a determination that a wise man would listen to even to the end of his life.

His gaze deepened on her face. "Okay, I trust you."

Warmth pooled in the edges of Nicky's eyes, igniting the corners of Luke's heart. "I trust you, too."

He dropped the stone and raised his hands. "Okay, Aaron. I'm unarmed. Let Nicky go."

"First, promise me you won't hurt Gracie." The young man's hands were shaking. Gracie was huddled against the cave wall, her knees pulled up to her chest. Her arms, a maze of scratches, were wrapped tightly around her stomach.

Luke dropped to his knees beside her. "I promise Gracie, I won't hurt you." His eyes searched the young woman's face. "Are you hurt?" Gracie shook her head.

He didn't believe her for a moment and glanced up at Aaron. "Look, Aaron, Nicky just put her own life on the line because she thinks you're going to do the right thing. She has first-aid training. She's used to dealing with injuries. So unless you really are the kind of guy who's planning to stab the one woman who could possibly help Gracie, let Nicky go now before I start to rethink my decision not to jump you."

The knife clattered to the cave floor and Nicky kicked it toward Luke. He palmed it smoothly, slid it into his belt and stood. "Thank you."

She slid over to Gracie and Luke. "Gracie? Honey? Where does it hurt? Are you injured?"

Gracie shook her head. Her face was pale and her skin was clammy.

Nicky glanced at Aaron. "When did she last eat? And how did you even get in here?"

"She won't eat." Aaron crossed her arms. "Not after the stew last night made people sick. I only had a bit of stew and I got really tired and spaced out. But Bear went full-on nuts. He started yelling that the trees were coming after him. He charged around tearing things apart. It was pretty scary. Gracie went to get you but you wouldn't wake up. So we hid until Bear stormed off for a while, grabbed everything good we could, and ran. We went into a cave in the forest and figured we'd hide until someone came to rescue us. We just kept crawling in deeper and deeper. Then the ground gave way and we fell down here. We couldn't climb back up. I found the Jet Ski and tried to steal it, but the guy in fatigues came back."

"Did you see the Hunter?" Luke asked. "Does he know you're here?"

Aaron shook his head. "No, we hid as far back as we could. He didn't come this far back."

Luke felt his eyes rise to the stone roof above his head. *Thank You, God, for that.* Nicky had been right that Aaron hadn't actually wanted to hurt her. These two terrified kids wouldn't have stood a chance against a genuine threat like the Hunter. *But how do I get all four of us out of here alive?* Even if he could steal the Jet Ski, it could only take two people maximum. He'd promised Nicky they wouldn't split up. Now it might be their only choice, whether she liked it or not.

Nicky was still trying to convince Gracie to unfold her arms and let her check for injuries.

"Look," Luke said. "If we're all going to get off this island alive we're going to have to be straight up and honest with each other. I'll tell you right now that the canoes have all been destroyed. We don't know what happened to everyone who took off yesterday or if your family members even made it to the mainland.

But based on the remains of a motorboat we found, it's possible the reason they're not back yet is that something's happened to them. Also, Russ is dead and probably Bear, too. They were shot with arrows."

Aaron gasped. Gracie whimpered.

Luke crossed his arms. "Now, I think it's high time the two of you were honest with us. We know Aaron slipped something into Gracie's hand just before we left Camp Spirit. Trevor went digging through people's bags and found your note, begging her not to come on this trip. So how about you tell us what's really going on?"

Aaron's eyes darted to Gracie's face. She pulled her arms tighter around herself. "Don't tell them anything."

Compassion filled Aaron's eyes. "Please, Gracie, I have to."

She shook her head. "You promised."

Nicky sighed. Then her fingers brushed Gracie's shoulder gently. "You're pregnant, aren't you?"

Sobbing broke over Gracie's body like a flood. Her head fell into her arms. Her body heaved.

Nicky wrapped both arms around Gracie's trembling shoulders, cradling her like a mother comforting an upset child. She pulled her close and murmured something into Gracie's hair that Luke couldn't quite hear. Gracie just shook her head. Nicky looked up at Aaron. "So, you're telling me you're in a cave, surrounded by food, and she hasn't eaten since *yesterday*?"

He nodded. "She barely touched her dinner. A couple of bites of bread, if that. We were fighting over it actually and she knocked the stew bowl out of my hands—which I should probably be thankful for."

Nicky sighed. "Her blood pressure had probably fallen through the floor. It's a wonder she hasn't passed out. Luke, please can you search that pile for something like an energy bar, and make sure it's sealed. There should be a red container of them in the bottom of the mini cooler."

"I'm on it." He searched around, fished one out and handed it to Nicky.

"Thanks." A grateful smile crossed her lips. She showed it to Gracie, opened it slowly in front of her and took the first bite herself. "Here, try this. As you can see, I just tried it and I can promise you it doesn't taste, smell or look tampered with. Whoever drugged us probably ground up sleeping pills into the stew. Something sealed like this is probably fine. Take small bites."

Then Nicky fixed her gaze back on Aaron. Frustration burned in her eyes. "What were you thinking, helping her hide something like this, on a trip like this? Do you have any idea how dangerous some of the more extreme sport activities could've been for her? This is exactly why I had you fill out health forms, so I could plan around things like this. It's bad enough that she lied and put her own life at risk, but for the baby's father not to step up—"

"It's David's, ma'am!" Aaron's hands rose. "Not mine. It's my brother's baby."

A long breath left Luke's lungs as a part of the puzzle he'd been staring at all weekend finally slotted into place. "So you've been trying to protect her?"

"And I told you not to!" Gracie's head snapped up. "David doesn't want me anymore, and he doesn't want anything to do with this baby."

Aaron's head shook. "You don't know that."

"Yes, I do! And so do you!" Fresh tears coursed down her face. She looked from Nicky to Luke in turn. "David's a player. I know for a fact he got his girlfriend pregnant and pushed her into terminating the pregnancy, because he wasn't going to let some unplanned kid derail his life. That was how he treated his *girlfriend*. We weren't even dating! We were just messing around, because I really liked him and hoped I could get him to like me, too. When I told David that I was in love with him, he told me that I meant nothing to him and I was just some girl he'd fooled around with. Then he stopped taking my calls and blocked me online."

"Did you tell him you were pregnant?" Nicky asked gently.

She sniffed. "Yeah. By text. He just texted back the contact details for a clinic. No message. Just the phone number and address. I texted that I'd made an appointment to terminate the pregnancy, and he wrote back 'Good.' But I never went for the appointment. I couldn't go through with it. I didn't want to."

"So, you came on this trip to talk to him?" Nicky's voice was soft and caring. It sounded a whole lot more gentle than Luke felt capable of being. David was lucky he wasn't there. Luke was tempted to punch him. "Was David upset you were here?"

"No. Worse." Gracie choked back sobs. "He just smiled his fake, plastic smile like I was nobody, and refused to make eye contact. Like I was just some girl he'd fooled around with and forgotten about, and expected me to be over it. It was like how much he'd hurt me hadn't even registered to him. He just doesn't care."

Nicky said something to Gracie, which again was too low for Luke to hear. Though he suspected it was David's brother, Aaron, who Nicky was trying to keep from overhearing. Then she tried again to coax her into taking a bite of food.

Luke's ears turned toward the mouth of the cave. Was it his imagination or did he hear a motor? He waited. But all he could hear was the sound of the water lapping against the cave's canvas door. "I'm sorry, Gracie," Luke said. "You deserve so much better. But we've got to figure a way out of here and soon. Trust me, I'll be first in line to talk some sense into David when you're back on shore."

Gracie's tear-stained eyes glared defiantly, first at Luke, then Aaron. "I already told Aaron, I'm not going to do that. Leave without me. What's the worst the Hunter's going to do? Kill me? Fine. I want to die. Don't you get that?"

Her voice rose. "My life is over, anyway. I don't want to get rid of the baby, but there's no way I can raise it by myself. Once word of this gets out, it's going to kill my mother's career. I can't do that to her. All her life she's been running on a major family values stance, and then her only daughter gets pregnant by some guy who won't step up? Now she's going to go into reelection with the news her own daughter is going to drop out of college to be an unwed teen mother?"

Her voice rose to a wail. "I can't do that!"

Luke's eyes met Nicky's. Gracie was panicking. She was spiraling out of control emotionally. Even though it was totally understandable under the circumstances, if she didn't calm down before the Hunter came back it could get them all killed.

"It's okay." Nicky ran her hand over the back of Gracie's hair. "You're a lot stronger than you know. You survived this long, didn't you? You wouldn't have run into the caves if you didn't want to live. Your mother loves you, and she'll be there for you. Maybe David will have smartened up and at least be willing to be in your baby's life—"

"You don't understand!" Gracie's shout echoed off the cave walls. "I've got a baby inside me, right now, that the father himself made clear he doesn't want! There is absolutely no way this goes well! None. There's no happy ending for me. There's no happy ending for this baby. Ever. Don't you get that?"

"I do." Luke dropped to his knees in front of the frightened young woman. "I get it."

"No, you don't get it. Nobody does." Gracie shook her head even harder now. She gulped back tears. "Please, just let the Hunter kill me. Put everyone out of their misery."

Luke took a long look at Nicky. Tears lit up the corners of her eyes. Dark shadows danced down the lines of her face, disappearing into waves of long dark hair. Her hand brushed against Luke's on the cold cave floor. He'd never seen someone more beautiful, inside and out.

Luke took a deep breath and looked at Gracie. "My mother was the kind of person who'd just drink and drink until she blacked out. When she was fifteen, she went to a party and passed out drunk. While she was unconscious, one of the boys at the party took advantage of her." He swallowed hard, forcing the words that he hated so much run like soothing water out of his soul. "That boy was my father."

Nicky squeezed his hand. He squeezed hers back.

"My mother raised me on her own. I'd like to think she did the best she could. But she never stopped drinking. Sometimes when she looked at me, it was as if all I was to her was a human reminder of the boy who'd attacked her and violated her. After a while, that's what she started telling me I was and all I'd ever be. Some worthless, evil piece of human trash like my father. And because that's what I believed about myself, that's how I acted. I got into fights. I stole things. I found and drank my mother's alcohol. I messed around with the pills in her medicine cabinet."

Nicky's fingers linked through his, weaving their hands together, the same way they used to hold hands when they were barely younger than the frightened young mother now curled up in front of them. Nicky's eyes filled with a look that made his heart catch painfully in his chest, and echo back with every beat of his own.

Oh, God, what were You doing? Why did You bring

Nicky back into my life? How am I ever going to handle the pain of letting her go?

Didn't she see? She could do so much better than a man like him. The blood of two very broken, damaged parents ran through his veins. That wasn't the kind of DNA Nicky deserved for the building blocks of her future.

"It took me nineteen years of being alive on this planet before I realized I was capable of being loved by someone," he added. "I lapped up that love she offered me like a parched man tasting water for the very first time. She deserved all the love a man could give back in return. But I was too broken to figure out how to love Nicky back. I wanted to love her. I really did. But all I could think to do was to run away from her before I screwed everything up and hurt her. Then it took many more years after that to even start to become the kind of man able to truly love another person in return."

A soft gasp left Nicky's lips.

For a moment the urge to wrap his arms around her was more than he thought he knew how to fight. But instead he pulled his hand away from Nicky's, crossed his arms over his chest and forced his eyes to look only at Gracie. He couldn't afford to lose focus. Not now.

"It was George Dale, of Camp Spirit, who showed me I had a choice in what kind of man I was going to be. George found me, high as a kite on stolen prescription drugs, practically crawling through his office in the lodge, with the Camp Spirit cash box clutched to my chest. George told me there was a God who loved me and would offer me a fresh start. A chance to be reborn and be the man God wanted me to be, not a person like either my father or mother. George gave me the very money from the cash box I'd tried to steal to pay my bail. He saved my life."

Aaron had crouched down with them. His hand brushed Gracie's shoulder. But neither Aaron's nor Gracie's stare left Luke's face for a moment. Slowly, Gracie's arms uncurled. Then she took a bite of the energy bar.

"So, trust me on this," Luke said. "Your life is not over. Your baby's life is not over. Regardless of what kind of father David does or doesn't decide to be, your child doesn't have to be doomed by that. You can give your baby the opportunity grow up in this world surrounded by a love, bigger and wider than you can probably even imagine—"

The thrum of a boat motor filled the air. Luke pressed one finger to his lips and then stood. The Hunter was back.

"Nicky, stay here with them and keep them safe. I'm going to go get that Jet Ski."

"No. Wait." Nicky grabbed his hand. "You said it yourself, neither of us is going to just go running off alone. We need to sit tight, stick together and plan what we're doing."

Her soft skin brushed against his fingers. The sound of the motor grew louder. Luke pulled away. "Yes, I know I said that. But that was before we'd found these two."

And that wasn't the only thing that had changed.

With every breath it was as though the air in his lungs now felt different, lighter and unsettling. He'd admitted feelings for Nicky that he'd never expected to spill. Yes, he'd done the right thing in saying what he had. It had been a story that Gracie had needed to hear. But somehow in the process of telling Gracie about his parents, Luke had opened his heart up far wider than he'd expected. Somehow wrenching his heart open and admitting the darkness about his parents and his past had subtly changed the energy between him and Nicky. And he didn't know how to change it back again.

"I've got Aaron's knife," Luke said. "One person alone is going to be a lot faster and more agile than two or four. If I go alone, I might be able to get the jump on him. Especially if he's still patrolling the island at two miles an hour. If I can hide somewhere, I can leap down and knock him right off before he even knows what's happening."

He didn't have much time. The motor noise was beginning to fade now. The Hunter was moving past. Hopefully he would loop all the way around the island looking for them. But, how long would it take until he was back?

Nicky stood and stretched. "Look, Luke, you're the one who convinced *me* that neither of us should head off anywhere without the other. You're the one who convinced me to trust you—"

"I know. But that was then. This is different." Luke started walking to the front of the cave. "I'm sorry if you can't see that, but there's not enough time to stop and have some big discussion about this. All that matters now is getting everyone out of here, home alive and back to our normal lives."

He strode through the cave. Then he slid into the water and waded toward the cave opening.

There was a splash behind him and he turned. Nicky had slid into the water behind him.

He could feel tension building at the back of his neck. "Please, just let me go and handle this alone. If you come with me, it's only going to put us both in even more danger."

Nicky's long wet hair framed her face, backlit by the flickering flashlight in the cave beyond. He half expected her to snap at him. An argument was something he could take. Instead, her hazel eyes filled with a depth of emotion that threatened to knock the air from his lungs. It wasn't a look of anger, frustration or even fear—but compassion.

"Look, I know things are really tense, really emotional and really dangerous right now," she said. "But that's all the more reason for you to slow down, take a deep breath and stick to our original plan. You're the one who convinced me not to keep pushing you away, because we're better in this together." Her voice dropped. "Please, don't just go running off alone like this."

"I have to. I'm just sorry you don't see it that way." Luke ran his hand along the camouflage canvas hiding the entrance of the cave, and listened. Silence. No, wait—a motor. Faint and growing fainter. He peered out. The Hunter was nowhere to be seen.

Luke pulled the canvas back and swam out, letting

it fall closed behind him. Nicky didn't follow him. He sighed and climbed up the wet, slippery island bank, his fingers and toes digging into the shallow rock. His knees banged against the sharp, jutting rocks. Fistfuls of scrubby grass threatened to give way under his grasp. Then he pulled himself up and onto the thick pine needles of the forest floor.

Luke crouched. The Hunter couldn't be that far ahead, not at the crawl he'd been going. Now it was the archer's turn to be the hunted one. Luke would slip along the water's edge, hiding behind the tree cover until he could catch sight of the Hunter on the water. Then Luke would get ahead of him and find a place where he could hide. When the Hunter's watercraft came into range, he would leap, catch him around the neck, pull him into the water and rip the mask from his face. He would finally bring his reign of terror to an end.

A large white boat loomed on the horizon. Rescue, perhaps. Well, by the time it got here, the Hunter would be in his custody.

Luke stood slowly and prepared to run. A cold, cruel chuckle wafted up from the water below him. *No. He can't have—* Luke looked down.

The Hunter was standing on the rocks below him, his bow aimed toward the cave where Nicky, Aaron and Gracie hid unaware and helpless. An ice-cold shiver spread down Luke's limbs like frost on a windowpane.

The Hunter had tricked him. The realization hit Luke like a blow to the gut and nearly brought him to his knees.

The Hunter drew his arrow back and aimed at the rock.

The arrow seemed to sizzle in the air as Luke ran for the edge, a prayer exploding through his heart. *Lord! Please! Don't let anyone be hurt because of my mistake!*

The Hunter's arrow flew. An explosion shook the ground beneath Luke's feet. He felt the earth buckle and give way as the entire rock face slid out from under him. His hands scrambled in vain for something to grab. Then Luke was falling, tumbling down in an uncontrollable cascade of dirt and rocks and trees.

His body fell into the water. His head hit rock. Earth and trees tumbled down the hill around him. The entrance to the cave disappeared completely, erased and buried, under the rock.

SIXTEEN

A rumble filled the air. The cave shook. Then, as Nicky watched, it was as if the entire cave roof above her folded in toward them. "Get back!"

She scrambled backward into the cave. Rock fell around her. Dirt filled her eyes. The flashlight went out. A deafening roar of falling earth echoed in her ears. She stumbled over camp equipment before Aaron grabbed her arm and pulled her deeper into the darkness. Her head smacked against the ceiling. She started to crawl. A cry for God's mercy filled her lungs.

Then silence.

Nicky coughed. She was lying on the ground, the granite floor pressing into her back. Her flashlight was dead. She blinked unseeingly into a wave of black and gray. Then a tiny spot of light flickered on beside her and the pale, pale faces of Aaron and Gracie swam into view. "Everyone okay?"

Gracie nodded. "Yeah. Think so."

Aaron managed a weak smile. "Nothing seems broken." A penlight glowed in his hands.

Nicky let her eyes close in prayer for a second. *Thank You, God.* Then she turned toward the solid wall of rock and debris, where just moments ago she'd watched Luke slip through the cave's mouth and out into the light of day. Where was Luke? Was he okay?

"Are we trapped?" Gracie's voice yanked Nicky's focus back to attention. The young woman sounded worried, but not panicked. Good. The calmer they stayed, the safer they would be.

"I hope not." Nicky kept her voice level. Prayers spun through her heart. She pulled herself up to crouching. Aaron's tiny pocket light flickered over the scene. Huge chunks of the rock littered the floor. The scattered pile of camp supplies was partially buried. Her flashlight still wouldn't turn on, so she shook it by her ear; all she could hear was the tinkling sound of broken glass. She pressed her fingers into her temples and tried to put together what she'd just seen. Luke had swum out of the cave. She'd waited, half hoping he'd come to his senses, turn around and come back. Then...

Laughter. She'd heard the sound of someone laughing. The same way the Hunter had laughed at them when he'd first ambushed them on the island two nights ago and laughed at her while she'd slept. The Hunter had probably booby-trapped the rock face above the cave with some kind of explosive that he could trigger easily, by arrow, from a distance. She sighed. They'd probably run right into a trap. "Have you guys tried climbing out of here the way you fell in?"

"Yeah," Aaron said. "But the drop was pretty steep.

We might as well have fallen down a well. We couldn't even get up a couple of feet without sliding back down."

"Okay, then, so we focus our energy on digging ourselves out this way." Nicky turned the broken flashlight over in her hands. The light bulb was shattered, but the flashlight itself was heavy, aluminum and fairly solid. Not a half-bad weapon, depending on what she met on the other side of the rock. She unscrewed the top of the flashlight, dumped out the batteries, then stomped on the open part as hard as she could. The metal flattened under her heel. Voilá, instant shovel.

"Okay," she said. "One of you go through the supplies, find something you can use to dig, then come join me up here. The other one gather up everything we can eat, drink, use to keep warm or start a fire with, and put it together in a bag. Just in case we're trapped awhile, I want to be prepared."

Especially as that little penlight wouldn't last forever. She ran her hand along the uneven wall of the cave-in, looking for a safe place to dig. Rock. Dirt. Grass. Tree roots. Pine needles. She pressed her lips together tightly. If the forest floor above had ended up inside the cave then the landslide must have been bigger than she'd realized. She dug her makeshift shovel into a patch of earth near the top of the mound.

"Where do you want me to dig?" Aaron clutched last night's stew ladle.

"Start over here. Pull away any large rocks that move easily. Just don't touch anything that looks like it's bearing weight. We don't want to risk the ceiling caving in any farther."

It was slow going and tedious. They chipped away at the mound in front of them and pried out rocks with their fingertips. For a moment she thought she heard a boat in the distance, but then the sound faded before she could even wonder if it belonged to a friend or a foe. Gracie joined in the digging after a while. The hole grew deeper. Suddenly there was a crash from the other side of the rock. Nicky froze. They heard another crack. A man grunted. A tiny sliver of light appeared between the rocks.

Then came a shout. "Hey! Anyone alive in there?"

"Yes!" *Thank You, God!* "Three of us!"

"Okay. Stand back!" Rocks tumbled toward them as the hole widened enough for a man's face to pop through.

"Neil?" She blinked. "What are you doing here?"

Well, if she was going to have a hallucination, the rival camp director probably wouldn't have been her first choice.

"Yup. Ace Sports to the rescue." Neil grinned. He chipped away at the hole. "George sent me. Sorry it took me a while to get to you. Had to moor the powerboat off shore a ways and paddle in on a life dinghy. Everyone doing okay in there?"

"Yeah." She glanced past him into the clear, blue sky beyond. "Have you seen Luke? Is he okay?"

"Yup! He's right here, sitting in the dinghy talking to police on my satellite phone. He was a bit banged up from the fall, but your boy's a tough one." Neil reached both arms through the hole. "Now grab my hands and I'll pull you out of there."

She stepped toward his outstretched hands. Then she stopped, as suspicion ruffled the back of her mind. "How do I know you're telling the truth?"

Neil blinked. "Seriously?"

Her fist tightened around her makeshift shovel. "I'm not going anywhere until I see Luke."

Neil pulled his arms back through the hole. "Okay, okay, have it your way." He disappeared from view. "Hey, Luke! Apparently Nicky wants some proof of life from you. Can you give her a shout?"

Nicky climbed up on a rock and peered through the hole. She blinked as the glare of the late-afternoon sun hit her eyes. Ace Sport's powerboat was moored off the island. An inflatable life-dinghy bobbed in the water beside the cave, with Luke sitting inside, cross-legged. With one hand he held Neil's high-tech satellite phone to his ear. With the other he turned one of the Hunter's arrows over slowly in his fingers. He looked exhausted.

"Hey!" Luke waved. "Yeah, I'm alive. The Hunter is nowhere in sight and I'm on with the police right now. Now hurry up and let's get out of here before the Hunter comes back."

Then Neil's face was back. "Luke told me our top priority should be getting a couple people to the hospital to get checked out. Seems like all of your campers are going to be passing through the emergency room. The whole lot of them that came back yesterday had the worst food poisoning I've ever seen. Showed up at the hospital so sick a couple of them even needed rehydration IVs. That's why I told George I'd come by today and check up on you."

"Is my mom okay?"

"What about David?"

Gracie and Aaron practically spoke over each other.

"All fine. Tabitha is still in hospital, but should be out today. She was one of the sickest. Martin was discharged this morning, and also had some kind of sprain. He went home, I think. I'm not too sure. I put David up in a chalet at Ace overnight. Trevor is still saying he's feeling too sick to go out on the water. So, like I said, I offered to motor out here and check up on things. So, you guys ready to get out of here, or what?"

Nicky stood back to let Aaron climb through first, then Gracie. Then, finally, she tumbled out of the hole and into Neil's waiting arms. He chuckled and set her down on the rock. "Here you go. Safe and sound."

"Thank you." A flush rose to her cheeks. But her eyes were set firmly on where Luke sat, still on the phone with the police. He'd barely looked at her.

Disappointment dripped into the recesses of her heart, even as she told herself she had no reason to be bothered. It only made sense that Neil had been the one to haul that last bit of rock away while Luke called the police. Obviously filing a police report was more important and pressing than simply standing outside a hole in the rock waiting to catch her, and it wasn't as if Luke wouldn't have helped dig, too, after he was off the phone. Still…

Luke put down the phone and stood carefully, bracing one foot on a rock. Her eyes searched his face, looking for any invitation to rush to him, to wrap her arms around his neck and tell him how relieved she was to see him safe. Instead, she ran her hands through her tangled hair, then down over her jeans. She was a mess. Every single part of her was streaked with dirt. "Luke, what happened? Are you okay?"

The glimmer of a smile briefly tugged at the corner of his lips. Then he sighed like a man four times his age.

"The Hunter got away. He'd rigged the cave to explode and the fall knocked me out cold. I'm so sorry, Nicky. I really should have seen it coming. Thankfully, Neil saw the explosion from a distance and made it here before the situation could get any worse. I'm just really glad you made it out okay." The arrow spun slowly in his hand. The arrowhead still looked so sharp it probably hadn't hit its intended target.

"You've got one of his arrows."

"Pulled it out of the water, I'm guessing it was intended as a parting shot after the rocks fell. The police are going to be out with a fleet of boats checking the shore for any glimpse of the Hunter. They'll be combing this island for clues and launching a full-scale manhunt."

Luke and Neil paddled the dinghy back to Ace Resorts' sleek white powerboat. They all climbed aboard and started for the mainland.

Gracie took the passenger seat at the front of the boat with Neil. Aaron stretched out in the very back of the boat, letting his arms fall over his face. In minutes, the twin had fallen asleep. Nicky and Luke sat side by side on plush leather seats facing backward. She watched as the island faded into the distance.

That was it? So, this was how their story ended. The Hunter had gotten away. Neil had been the one to play knight in shining armor. And she and Luke were back to sitting in a boat, not even knowing what to say to each other.

Luke's gray-blue eyes stared almost blankly out over the white spray of water spreading out behind them. It was the same faraway look he'd had years ago when they were younger, on the day before he'd tried to steal the cash box and run away. His arm was just inches away from hers. The fingers on his right hand hung in midair beside hers. It would be so easy to touch him, to just reach her hand out to squeeze his arm or to loop her fingers through his.

She sat back. Well, what had she been thinking was actually going to happen at the end of all this? That Luke was going to leap from the cave, singlehandedly defeat the Hunter, then pull her deeply into his arms and promise to stay by her side forever?

An unexpected giggle almost slipped through her lips. All that sounded exactly how eighteen-year-old Nicky would have imagined the story ending. But life wasn't a cotton-candy fantasy. At least now God had given her a glimpse of the man Luke had become, which was a far better memory of him to be left with.

Well, Lord, I never thought I'd say this, but thank You that Luke broke my heart and ran from me all those years ago. He needed to grow up so much, and I wasn't mature enough to take it. Seeing him now, seeing everything he's become, I just want to say thank You for the man he became without me. And thank You for the woman I became without him.

The boat slowed. She opened her eyes. The burned-out shell of Camp Spirit's main lodge loomed between the trees. Speaking of misjudging, she probably owed Neil an apology, too. She swiveled in her seat and tapped him on the shoulder. "Hey, I'm really sorry I was so suspicious when you rescued us from that cave."

Neil shrugged. "Consider it forgotten. Going through everything you'd gone through, I'm not surprised if you went a little loopy." He steered the boat past Camp Spirit and farther down the coast toward the largest of Ace Resort's boathouses. "I promise, the fact you suspected me of being a serial killer won't have any impact on our working relationship."

She forced a smile. Nice try. It would take a lot more than getting trapped in a cave-in and hunted by a killer to convince her to abandon George and quit her job at Camp Spirit. "Ha-ha. Thanks, but I've told you before I'm not about to come work for Ace Sports. Camp Spirit is going to need a lot of help recovering from everything that's happened this weekend, and I intend to stick with it and help see it through."

"Yeah, I know." Neil cut the engine. He draped one arm over the steering wheel and glanced back at her. "That's why I told George I'd be willing to mentor you through the whole, big transition. In fact, George asked me just yesterday if I'd be willing to sit down and give you any advice I had on dealing with the new owners."

"New owners? What new owners?" She couldn't

have sat up straighter or more suddenly if Neil had stabbed an actual dart in her spine.

Luke spun around in his seat, too. Was this what George had summoned Luke up here for? Had the secret thing George needed to discuss with Luke been nothing more than asking him to cover the story about George's plans to sell the place?

"What on earth are you talking about? I'd know if George had been showing the place around to prospective buyers. In fact, he told me specifically he was looking for a few key investors, to keep the place running as it was. So I presumed he was planning on hanging on to it a while longer."

Neil shrugged again. "Well, I heard it from the old man himself. And it's not just one new owner. They're apparently taking it to a shareholder model just like Ace Sports. So I hope you're prepared to go from dealing with one nice old man to answering to a whole room full of money-hungry task masters. Trust me, it isn't fun." He turned back to the shoreline. "Don't say I didn't try to warn you. I told you Friday I thought something was up with him. But in my experience, staff is usually the last to know."

Staff. And here George had always made her feel like family instead of someone he just paid to manage camp counselors, teach kids how to paddle canoes and make sure people kept the cabins clean. Then why did George put her through the charade of taking a whole group of people to the island? Was he hoping the likes of Bear and Russ had enough money to buy a few shares?

Her chest felt so tight she could barely breathe. The sound of her own pounding heart filled her ears. No wonder Trevor had been so arrogant when she'd caught him searching bags. He must have known a sale was in the works and that as soon as George signed the paperwork, Trevor was finally going to get his quick cash payday.

Luke was leaning forward now. He was listening intently, with a smile on his lips.

Hang on—Luke thought this was a *good idea*? Tears sprang to her eyes. She blinked hard and didn't let them fall. George had betrayed her. The camp was going to be divvied up among a group of money-hungry strangers. And Luke was actually *happy* about it? George and Luke were the two men she'd cared about the most in her entire adult life. Now she was left wondering how much she actually mattered to either of them.

Thank You, God, that George was finally selling the camp! Luke glanced to the sky, though, as the prayer of relief filled his chest. It was time George let himself retire and relax, not to mention, finally, Nicky would be working for the kind of place able to make her dreams come true. Not to mention, she would be safe. Sure, it would probably be hard on her. But if anyone could handle the challenge it was Nicky.

Neil leaned back in his seat, steering the boat with one hand while talking over his shoulder. "Can't blame him really," Neil went on. "It's not like Trevor was ever going to want to run the place. It was pretty obvious that kid was just putting in time until he could get enough cash together to take off again. In fact, when Trevor was on a supply run back to camp yesterday, George told me straight-up that a big part of his main motivation for stepping aside now was that he wanted to give Trevor his inheritance while he was still young enough to go make something of his life. That's one seriously nice dad Trev's got."

Neil clicked a remote and the big white doors of the boathouse rolled open. Three boats sat inside. They practically gleamed. Neil patted Nicky's shoulder. "Don't look so glum, kiddo. I'm sure it goes without saying that if your new board of directors don't like you, or you don't like them, I'll definitely suggest bringing you on here as my right-hand gal."

He docked the boat. They disembarked and Neil led them through a maze of Ace Sports' buildings and chalets to the parking lot.

Nicky trailed behind the group. Luke dropped back and matched her stride. "Look, I know this whole thing must come as a shock, but George has a point wanting to sell sooner rather than later. He's not as young as he used to be and the place needs a lot of work. If he's ready to pack it in and move on to retirement, then good for him."

Her eyes grew wide. "So you're *defending* him?"

"Defending George's right to sell the camp he built and retire? Yeah. Of course. It's his baby. Not yours."

She stopped walking so suddenly it took him a few steps to realize she was no longer keeping up. He stopped and turned back. She'd crossed her arms in front of her chest. "Unbelievable."

She'd muttered the word so low he wasn't sure if she was talking to him or to herself. The rest of the group had stopped now and was watching them. Luke waved them on. "Neil, how about you go ahead and take Aaron and Gracie to the hospital? Nicky and I can grab our vehicles from Camp Spirit and meet you there."

Aaron and Gracie hesitated, but Nicky waved at them, too. "It's a great idea. Neil's got a really comfortable sports utility vehicle. I'll meet up with you at the hospital in a bit."

Hopefully, Nicky would calm herself down a whole lot before then. Level heads were what was needed right now, and her hands were clenched so tightly she looked ready to scream. The others kept walking. Luke waited until they disappeared from view, then he walked back to Nicky.

"Look, I get it," he said softly. "You love Camp Spirit and are afraid to imagine working anywhere else. But if these past few days have showed you anything, it's that the camp is in worse shape than you realized and needs far more than you and George are able to put into it."

She snorted. "That some kind of joke? Why would you say that? Because we were sabotaged and attacked by the Hunter?"

"Honestly? Yes. Partially."

Now the fury building behind her eyes looked ready to erupt into a shout. But she pressed her lips together and kept her voice level. "Are you kidding me? You're blaming us, blaming *me*, for the fact someone sets fire to our lodge, vandalizes the island and kills two people?"

"That's not what I'm saying." How could she not get this? "Stop making everything personal, and don't twist my words.

"No, of course no one is to blame for that evil criminal's actions but himself. But *if* you'd owned more motorboats and bigger boats, we might not have gotten stranded in the first place. If anyone on our camping trip had owned a state-of-the-art satellite phone like Neil's, we'd have been able to call the police right from the island. If Camp Spirit had a larger off-season staff, someone might have rescued us sooner. If the camp had invested some serious money in revitalizing the waterfront and doing more to the caves than just slapping up some No Entry boards then maybe the Hunter wouldn't have been able to hide as long as he did."

She tossed her head. "You *are* blaming Camp Spirit, because we aren't wealthy enough to afford fancy toys and haven't managed to get charity status yet. You're making us sound like a death trap." She flung her arms open wide then practically spun in a circle. "So, *this* should be my future? Forget about running a small, special camp which works to change the lives of people who need help the most, like those troubled teens we talked about this morning. Instead, I should accept being just another cog in a gleaming sports machine for the rich and elite, where we pick and choose campers based on how far they can throw a ball and how much money they've got. Forget about kids who need a second chance. Forget about kids who are poor, or unco-ordinated, or misfits and outsiders who don't fit in."

Luke crossed his arms. "You're being absolutely ridiculous."

"Am I? You heard Neil. You go ask him what it's like to work for some commercially minded board of directors, beholden to hundreds of shareholders, whose only priority is figuring out how to use what could be the most important summer of a kid's life as nothing but another money-making opportunity. How sad."

"No, what's sad is how little you believe in George if you're this quick to take everything Neil says at face value." He could feel heat building at the back of his neck. "I know you were hoping this sponsorship trip might mean George could hang on to this place for a couple more years. But if the next heart attack ends up being fatal, Trevor probably won't put anywhere near enough thought and care into finding buyers who respect George's faith and priorities.

"So, rather than seeing it as some kind of personal betrayal, maybe you should just recognize that George has the right to give up, say goodbye to this place and move on with his life. Sometimes the kindest thing to do is pack it in and walk away."

"Well, you're the expert on saying goodbye—" Nicky swallowed her words as a group of Ace staff came out of a building. She turned to the right and cut through the buildings. He followed. She kept her lips closed tightly together until they reached the path to Camp Spirit.

"I'm sorry. That came out a lot harsher than I intended. But you don't know what it's like. You're an outsider who's barely set foot here. You were never a camper, a counselor or a volunteer. You've never seen a kid's face light up the first time they pick up a paddle or gotten caught in the happy stampede of people racing to the lodge for breakfast."

Their footsteps crested the hill. The setting sun brushed across Camp Spirit in a wave of golden light, deepening to red at the horizon.

"Yes, maybe all I was ever going to get was one or two more summers. But every day this place has campers in it is a chance to change someone's life. George, our counselors, our staff, me, the campers... people poured themselves into this place and got so much back in return. So if I don't think you should get a vote, it's not personal. It's because you've never invested anything in this place, let alone an actual piece of yourself."

He could tell she meant it rhetorically. But still his shoulders stiffened. "Yes, actually, I have. I gave everything I had to this camp you claim I know nothing about."

Her head shook. "No, not the way I mean—"

"Nicky! Listen!" His hands touched her shoulders, turning her toward him. "Listen to what I'm saying. I *have.* I've invested every single cent I could into this place you love. You told me some mystery donor friend of George's gave you a giant lump sum of hundreds of thousands to help this place stay afloat? That was me."

SEVENTEEN

He watched as her golden eyes grew wide. Her face paled. Nicky's lips parted, but no words came out.

"I'm sorry." Luke grabbed her hand. "I didn't mean to just drop something like that on you. George and I agreed it would remain our secret. But yes, that big donation that kept you going was from me."

"No, I can't believe you." She was shaking, but he couldn't tell whether it was more from anger or shock. "I can't believe after everything we're going through, I'm still discovering lies. You told me straight-up that you didn't have money—not big, serious life-changing money. You told me that you were just a sport's reporter."

"I didn't lie." A long sigh left his chest. "I just didn't tell you, because I didn't want you treating me any differently. I definitely don't have money like that anymore…

"When I was twenty-two, a lawyer showed up at my tiny little apartment and told me my father had died and left me everything. I didn't know my father. Never met him. Definitely didn't want anything to do with him. But apparently he knew who I was.

"I can only guess that my mother wasn't a total stranger to him and when she had me he'd found out about it somehow. For all I know she called him up drunk one night and told him herself. Maybe they talked throughout my childhood. I don't know. They both had substance abuse problems and she wouldn't tell me anything about him. But he named me as his only heir—to his house, his life insurance policy, his savings, everything."

"I'm sorry, that must have been hard." She was still holding his hand.

He looked down. Her toes were barely an inch away from his. "It was incredibly hard. I ignored it for months. Eventually, I hired someone to clear out his house, sell his property and basically liquidate his life. Then, one day, while I was still sorting out my father's estate, Mom took an overdose and suddenly I had her estate to deal with, as well."

His eyes closed as he remembered the police showing up to inform him. Those were some of the darkest days of his life. "If it hadn't been for my boss, my co-workers, my church and for George, I don't think I'd have made it." He pulled his hand out of hers.

"Anyway, Mom didn't really own much of value—just a small run-down house. But the market happened to be really good in that part of town and a developer wanted the land. Plus there were envelopes of money from my father stashed under her mattress. Thousands of dollars of, I'm guessing, guilt money he'd apparently sent over the years to help her and me. She'd never even opened any of the envelopes. There were no notes inside, just cash."

Luke turned and walked toward the tree line. The setting sun cascaded through the treetops beneath him. "So there I was, barely twenty-three years old, in possession of the spoils of my parents' lives, desperately knowing I needed to put the past behind me and move on with my life. Thankfully, I had a good job and a place to live. I didn't have any intention of going to university and, considering my family history, I thought having a family of my own was completely out of the question…"

A hand brushed his arm. He turned. She'd followed him. "So, you gave it all to George?"

He rolled his shoulders back. "Believe me, I didn't want anything to do with it. I didn't want even one single cent going toward something I was going to have to ever see again. Donating it to Camp Spirit felt right. I felt like I owed George my life."

She nodded slowly. "So that's why you never wanted to volunteer here or to talk to the campers. Maybe that's even why you're happy to see this place sold."

He turned toward her. "What on earth are you talking about? That's not it at all."

"Are you sure?" The anger had faded completely from her face. Instead, her eyes were filled with compassion and a willingness to understand. "Your gift kept this place alive. You have to have looked around here and known that cabins have roofs, boats are running, obstacle courses are standing—all because of that money you gave. I saw you frown when you first got out of your car on Thursday. Maybe it was because you knew your parents' money helped build this."

His shrug was so big his arms practically did a backstroke. "If I frowned it was because seeing the lodge again reminded me of how immature and selfish I'd once been. Even George reminded me of that when I pulled him out of the fire. Bottom line is George was wrong to think I should be up here playing camp counselor. I'm not the kind of man anyone would want kids looking up to. Maybe even he gets that now."

Her eyes closed for a moment, as though she was listening to a piece of music only she could hear. "You're wrong." She looked up into his face. "You're exactly the kind of person kids like that need. I've seen you in action. I've listened to you. I'm alive because of you. I heard what you said to Gracie and Aaron—"

He bristled. "I only told them that because I didn't want Gracie to give up on herself."

"But I'm supposed to just stand here and listen to you give up on yourself? Maybe it wasn't just guilt that made you donate that money. Maybe deep in your heart you really believed in what we were trying to do. And if I have any hope of talking George out of this sale, you are exactly the kind of person I need by my side. If you and I went to George together, I know he would listen."

"I appreciate what you're trying to do, but I'm not your champion here." Luke stuffed his hands into his pockets. "I totally respect George's decision and I'm not about to argue with him about something that's ultimately none of my business."

All he'd ever promised was to get Nicky home safely. His job here was done. Now it was time to book into a hotel, get into some clean clothes, call the police to see if they wanted anything more from him and check in at work.

Nicky's slim shoulders sagged like a deflated balloon. "So you're giving up."

"You can't give up something that was never yours to begin with."

Her eyes were still locked on his face—beautiful, vibrant, asking him for something neither of them had the courage to put into words. It rattled him. Part of him wanted to make her see sense. Part of him wanted to kiss her. Part of him even wanted to be nineteen again and come running through the woods to the place he knew she was waiting for him, instead of breaking into the lodge and running away.

"What do you want from me, Nicky? Really? If you're thinking something, just come out and say it."

A sad smile crossed her lips. "What I want is to never have trusted my hopes and my dreams to George or to you." She raised her head toward the horizon. "Well, I'm going to go hit my cabin, call the police and get changed—not to mention pray for a bit. Then I'm going to head over to the hospital. Will I see you there?"

"Probably not." His heart pricked with every beat, as if there was a splinter stuck in his chest. He should say goodbye properly this time. He should tell her how thankful he was to have been able to get to know her again. He needed to tell her how he admired her and how he hoped she'd have an amazing future. Maybe even admit how deeply he suspected he was going to miss her. But to say something like that would be to acknowledge that this was their final goodbye and he knew he wasn't coming back.

She stepped toward him. His heartbeat raced. Her hand brushed his chest. "Goodbye, Luke Wolf, and thanks for everything."

"Do you want me to walk you back to camp?"

"No, thanks." She stepped back then turned toward the horizon. "I'm okay on my own."

Nicky's footsteps stumbled through the woods back into Camp Spirit. Long shadows crossed the ground under her feet. She felt numb. Part of her wanted to just curl up under a tree and cry. But if she did that, she might not get up again. These old familiar buildings had been part of her world her entire adult life. She'd hammered some of these nails. She'd shingled some of these roofs. She knew every root and rock under her feet. There was no way she'd let this place go without a fight.

The kids who came here were the kind who needed a place to belong and someone to believe in them. Every summer they stayed open allowed them to reach a few more. Maybe George no longer had enough steam to keep it going. But to just sell it out from under her like this? One didn't give up on things that mattered just because they were in a bad place and needed fixing. She'd get washed up, go see George and they'd sort this out.

The hollow husk of the burned-out lodge loomed

ahead. The few remaining crossbeams stretched bare above her, like the skeleton of a mythical beast. Yellow warning tape lay twisted on the ground, spilling out from the wood beams. A mountain of boards and debris filled what was once the lodge floor. A figure was standing on top of the heap in the middle of the destruction.

"George?"

It looked as though her boss had been discharged from hospital and was checking out the remains of the lodge for himself. Words bubbled out of her mouth as she tripped and picked her way over the police tape. "I can't tell you how thankful I am to see you. Neil told me what you're planning. Please, don't sell. I know the camp is in trouble. I know the situation is bleak. But, please, don't just give up. Not like this."

He turned. She was wrong. It wasn't George. It was Trevor.

"Oh, hey! I'm sorry. I thought you were your father." Her feet slid to a stop just inside the threshold of what was once the dining-room door. She stepped through carefully. Scorched gray wood crumbled to ashes beneath her boots. "How are you doing? Neil told me you all came down with food poisoning."

"Yeah." He nodded slowly. "Pretty bad, actually. I was out for a few hours there."

"Sorry to hear it. The dinner stew was laced with some kind of sleeping pill. I'm guessing the Hunter did something to the soup, too."

Trevor stared at her for a long moment. "You call him 'the Hunter'? Interesting. I didn't realize you'd given him a name." He walked down the heap toward her. Broken glass and charred pieces of ceiling tile snapped and cracked under his feet. He stopped while still a full head above her. "Did Neil actually tell you my father is thinking of *selling* this place?"

"Yes. Well, no… Not exactly." She paused as her brain scrambled backward to remember Neil's exact words. "He told me that your dad was stepping down and there were going to be new owners. We never discussed specifics."

Rather, her worst fears had taken over at that point. Then again, Neil had also said that George wanted Trevor to get his inheritance sooner rather than later, and she could hardly expect Trevor to disagree with that.

"Look, I get it," she added. "Your father's health is failing. Our financial situation is terrible and there's a lot of work to be done. But still, he can't give up and sell it off."

Once again Trevor watched her for a long moment. It was disconcerting. "Why not?"

"Because the value of a camp like this is more than just the value of the land it sits on. Yes, I know to you it's probably just some business your dad built that you have no interest in. But this place changes people's lives for the better and we owe it to our past and future campers to at least try and preserve that legacy."

"Huh." Trevor's head titled to the side. "See, I'd think whatever happy feelings people had for this place were destroyed along with the lodge and buried along with the bodies. There is no way my father will ever be able to recover from the stigma of everything that's happened this weekend." His hand swept through the air over the debris at his feet. "This is the end, my friend. Our reputation is dead. There's no coming back. No amount of fresh paint is ever going to make parents want to send their kids into a death trap. Dad's only chance now is to give up and sell it fast to some developer who'll give him a quick wad of cash then raze the land."

Sounded as though he'd given it a lot of thought. But that didn't mean he was right. Trevor might have been George's only son. But that didn't mean for one moment he'd ever understood.

She took a step toward him. "You're wrong. Yeah, it will be tough. But not impossible. Because Camp Spirit isn't just a summer camp. It's alive and living, like a heart. Drawing people in, making them bolder and stronger, and then sending them back out into the world again." Yes, it was exactly like that. A little, broken, battered extension of God's heart. "Do you have any idea how many people love this place? We could get on the phones and start calling former campers. People would step up and help. One might even make George a better offer—"

"Hang on." Trevor held up a hand. "But what if we could go to the hospital right now, hand my dad some sale papers and tell him we should take the money and run? You *wouldn't* have my back?"

"No, I'm sorry."

He blinked. "Not even if there was a cash bonus in it for you?"

She shook her head. "Not if it's to some developer who'll just level the place. I'd tell him to find the kind of owners who will honor Camp Spirit."

"Really? Are you sure I can't convince you otherwise?"

She grinned. "No, you really can't."

He swore under his breath. "Shame." He slid a gun from behind his back and pointed it at her face. "I was really hoping I wouldn't have to kill you."

EIGHTEEN

Trevor aimed the gun directly between Nicky's eyes. He walked down the debris pile toward her like a dragon leaving his hoard. The gun was as steady as stone in his grasp. She was face to face with the Hunter one more time, and something told her that this time he had no intention of letting her go.

"Where's your bow and arrows?"

He chuckled darkly. "Elsewhere. While they were rather perfect for a place like the island—silent, stealthy, extra bit of fear factor—I think this calls for something a little less elegant."

Nicky's hands rose. In her mind's eye she imagined slipping her very life into them and lifting it up toward heaven. *Dear Lord, I don't know if I'm going to get out of this alive. Whatever happens now, please, please hold me safe in Your care.*

"You have no reason to do this," she said. "Neil told me that your father is selling now specifically because he wants to give you your inheritance. You're already getting everything you want. All I could possibly do is encourage George to delay the sale long enough to find the right buyer. Either way all the money from this place still goes to you."

"You have no idea what's really going on, do you?" Trevor scowled. "Neil got it all wrong. My father isn't selling the camp on the open market. He's selectively selling off shares—for far less than a developer would pay—to three or four handpicked investors who will help him keep running this place the way he wants. That's what this whole weekend charade was about... Seeing if he can find the right people who'll sit around in some table like the king's counsel. Yap, yap, yapping away, while they divide up what's rightfully *mine*." He flapped his fingers together like a bird's mouth.

A deep sigh of regret washed through her heart. She should have known George would never throw Camp Spirit to the jackals or the highest bidder. *Lord, forgive me.*

"So this is all about money and the size of your inheritance? You knew a developer would give you more money for the land than the kind of owners your father would choose, so you decided to commit murder to get a bit bigger slice of the pie."

"A bit bigger?" His voice rose. "You really have no clue, do you? He told me what he was planning. And when I thought he couldn't really be serious about going through with it, I found it had all been spelled out, for years, in his will in the loft!" His hand rose to empty space above their heads. "He's reduced my inheritance to thousands. That's all. A few lousy thousand, when the whole thing should rightly be mine.

Oh, he's asking the investors to chip in far less than this land is worth, and even then asking they invest all that money right back into the camp. But this property and that island—my rightful inheritance—is worth *millions*." His eyes narrowed. "And, yeah, I think several million dollars is worth sabotaging an obstacle course, setting fire to a lodge and smashing up a few canoes for. Not to mention faking some pretty serious food poisoning."

"Trevor, you *murdered* people."

"It's not like I *planned* to. Russ was going to stop me from sabotaging the canoes. And I had no idea Bear had a gun on him. I'd already checked his bag and it's not like you were going to let me pat people down for weapons." He rolled his eyes. "Not particularly happy about how it all played out on the island, especially as I was only really aiming for a bit of scare tactics and terror. But I'm not going to be so sloppy with you."

He crossed the floor and stopped, just outside her reach. "See, I know you, Nicky. If I play nice, you're only going to try something stupid like knock this gun out of my hand. This time, things are happening my way." A cold grin spread across his face. "You're going to turn around, raise your hands and walk where I tell you. Otherwise, I will make you suffer. Got it?"

"Perfectly." The Hunter's gun dug deep into the small of her back as Trevor marched her up through the woods. Nicky's hands were linked at the top of her head. Her lips moved in silent prayer. *Help me, Lord.* Their path wound up the woods. "You're taking me to the lookout."

"Seems appropriate, yes." Trevor pushed the pistol deeper into her skin. "Seems like a logical place for you to commit suicide. I'm going to walk you right up to the edge, turn you toward Ace Sports and fling you right down onto the roof of their shiny new gym. Make them worry about cleaning up a body for once." He giggled until his voice cracked.

Nicky froze. Once they reached the lookout cliff it didn't matter which direction she fell. There'd be nothing but a steep fall on all sides. Whether she went down over the jagged rocky shore of Camp Spirit or the buildings of Ace Sports, there was no way she'd survive the fall.

Trevor cuffed her on the back of the head, sending tears flooding to her eyes. She gritted her teeth. "Please. It doesn't have to end like this. It's not too late to choose to be a better man, to be someone worthy of your father's legacy." There was no answer except for the sound of his footsteps crunching on the forest floor behind her. "Please, Trevor. You said yourself you never intended anyone to die—"

He laughed. "Yeah, because I knew that if someone was murdered here it would sink the property value. You think I didn't do my homework? A few bad accidents and some sabotage by a random trespasser are the kinds of things which would tank my father's plan, maybe even make you willing to quit, without actually impacting how much I could get for the place. Murder, though, kills a property's value. Prospective buyers get squeamish about stuff like that. It's bad enough I'm almost certainly going to get less for the island now."

They reached the top of the hill. The lookout cliff was only steps away now. He was taking her to die in the very place she'd gone to for years when she needed to find peace with God. "I'm not going to jump for you. Or let you pretend it was suicide." Slowly Nicky turned toward her attacker. "If you're going to kill me, you're going to shoot me."

Hatred filled the dark recesses of his eyes, sending a chill down her spine. The pleasant mask had slipped away from his face and the fake grin was gone, leaving nothing behind but an angry, vicious, childish narcissist, determined to take what he'd decided he was owed. He screamed so loudly his mouth foamed. "Turn around! Now!"

She stepped toward him. The barrel of his gun brushed against her forehead. She focused her eyes on the miserable man behind the weapon. "No. I'm done playing your sick game."

He grabbed for her throat. His fingers dug into the soft flesh deeper and deeper until the breath left her lungs and intense pain made darkness fill her eyes. "You are going to do exactly what I say, because I'm going to hurt you, and hurt you, and keep hurting you until you do." Her legs gave way, sending her to her knees in the dirt.

He leaned down, until his mouth was level to her ear. "I've given you more than enough chances!" he shouted, sending pain echoing through her ears. "I kept trying and trying not to kill you, because I hoped I might be able to use you to argue sense into my father. I hoped you'd get scared or upset enough you'd take a buyout and quit. That would have helped me. More than you know. But you had to be difficult." His fingers latched onto her hair, yanking her up. "Now, you're going to die and I'm going to claim what's mine."

Luke's hands gripped the steering wheel. He'd never made a U-turn that fast before. But the whole way down the highway his chest had been aching as if he'd somehow left a piece of himself behind at the camp and his heart was now struggling to beat without it. He couldn't let it end this way. George was like a father to him. Nicky set his heart on fire. He should have agreed to go with her to the hospital to talk to him. Not to take sides. But to support them both.

Besides, he couldn't just run away without even making an attempt to let Nicky know how he felt. She deserved better than that, and maybe so did he. Either way, he wasn't that boy who just ran anymore.

He pulled into the Camp Spirit campgrounds and froze. Trevor's truck was parked right behind Nicky's, pinning her vehicle in so she couldn't pull out. The hair on the back of his neck stood on end.

He got out and circled Trevor's truck. There was something under the front seat, in a case and mostly hidden under a tarp. But even then there was no mistaking the telltale shape. It was a hunting bow. Luke took a deep breath and glanced up just in time to see two figures disappear toward the lookout.

No signal on his cell phone. No time to go get help. The sun was moments away from setting completely.

If he lost sight of them in the woods, he might never figure out where they'd gone.

He took a deep breath and grabbed his handmade six-foot wooden bow from his trunk. All he'd brought for arrows were the lightweight, recreational ones he used for shooting paper targets. Not much use against a killer. The lone hunting arrow he'd plucked from the water slid into his quiver. It was time to hunt the Hunter.

He sprinted through the woods as silently as he could, as quickly as he dared, as his eyes adjusted to the darkness. The wind whistled in the branches around him. He could hear the babble of voices ahead. Then Nicky cried out in pain. The sound hit him like a punch to the gut, pushing him faster.

He reached the lookout path. His footsteps slowed to silent as the trees parted just enough to let him see in the soft light of the rising moon. Nicky was down on her knees. With one hand Trevor yanked her hair so hard she winced. With the other he held a gun to her head. They were so close to the edge now that one wrong move on her part, any attempt she made to fight back, would send them both tumbling over the edge to their deaths.

"May God have mercy on you, Trevor," he heard her say.

Trevor snarled.

Luke slotted his arrow into the string.

Trevor clicked the safety off and leveled the gun between her eyes.

Luke pulled the string back, feeling every beat of his heart infuse all his strength into his one and only shot.

Nicky's eyes closed.

Trevor's finger brushed the trigger.

"Let. Her. Go." Luke stepped through the trees. "It's over."

Trevor turned. "So the miserable little beggar returns once again to steal what's mine. You think you can just sneak in and steal my camp out from under me?"

Steal his camp? Was he delusional? "I don't know what you're talking about. I'm not stealing anything from you." Not that it was probably much use using logic against a madman holding a gun to Nicky's head.

"Liar!" The Hunter barked a laugh that turned into a snarl. "You think I don't know who I'm talking to? You're still nothing but the worthless piece of human garbage that crawled into my father's life. The thief. The runaway. The addict who was sick on the floor. You didn't deserve my father's compassion. He should have left you to die in the gutter like the sewer trash you are."

The bitter, jealous words hit Luke's ear with a cold dead clang. He'd heard those lies too many times before. He'd told himself those lies. But now he was going to fix his gaze on the first person who'd ever truly loved him—and remember that he truly was the man he'd seen mirrored in her eyes.

"Trust me, I've not forgotten where I came from, or just how hard I fought to become a better man. But, no, I was never worthless. No one is. It's just that some of us play the roles that we're taught until someone helps us to see who we really are, as Nicky did for me." Luke focused his sights and pulled the arrow farther back. "Last chance."

"Like you're able to stop me." Trevor cocked the gun. "You took what's mine. Now I'm going to destroy what matters to you."

The arrow flew. There was the whistle of the shaft brushing through the wind then a scream as it sliced into the back of Trevor's hand.

The gun went off. The bullet shot into sky.

Nicky kicked the gun from Trevor's hand and it clattered over the cliff. Then came the echo of it hitting the ground far, far below.

"Luke!" She ran toward him.

"No! You don't get to win!" Trevor wheeled around. His fist swung through the air. The blow caught Nicky on the temple. It knocked her over the edge. Then she was gone.

NINETEEN

Trevor had thrown Nicky off the cliff. Luke felt his heart stop. His knees threatened to crumble beneath him. Silence filled the air, as if waiting for her to fill it with a scream. There was no way she'd survive the fall. *Lord, please, I don't want to face this world without her—*

"Luke!" Her voice rose from below him, sending joy soaring through his chest. "Help!"

Trevor turned toward the sound. Luke decked him. One decisive blow struck Trevor on the jaw. The Hunter crumpled to the ground.

"Nicky!" Luke ran to the edge of the cliff. "I'm here!"

There she was, a few feet down, clinging with both hands to a tiny branch, not much thicker than his finger, while her feet searched desperately for their grip.

"It's okay." He dropped to his stomach and reached over the ledge for her, stretching down his bow for her to grab. "I've got you."

She grabbed hold and held on tight. "You came back for me."

"Of course I did." A smile crossed his lips as he pulled her to safety.

"I can't believe you made that shot."

He chuckled. "Told you that you'd inspired me to learn a thing or two."

Luke slung his bow over his shoulder as he and Nicky walked down the hill to call the police from Camp Spirit's emergency phone. They'd left Trevor in the woods, conscious and tied so tightly to a tree there was no chance of his escape.

As they stood in silence, waiting for the authorities to arrive, the moon rose high in the sky above them. Her head drifted onto his shoulder. His fingers linked through hers.

"Neil was wrong about George, and so was I," she said as she leaned against Luke's chest. Her eyes drifted from the shabby boathouse, past the remains of the lodge and out over the cabins, disappearing into the thick, untamed trees.

"Yes, he's planning on giving up this place. But not recklessly. It's more like he's choosing a small handful of buyers who will work together to make it great. Actual investors, who want to share in this place. And maybe a group of co-owners working together is better than entrusting ownership of all this to just one man or woman, especially if they share George's vision of turning the camp into a thriving charity."

Wise. It sounded as though George had found a way to let go of this place while making sure it was on the right footing for the future. Luke ran his hand down her arm. "And how do you feel about that?"

"I don't know. A bit better. Relieved, but also uncertain. Look, even if I'd ever been the kind of person who had money to buy into a place like this, I'm not the kind of person who wants to be involved in the business side of things. The person who runs the business doesn't get to be the person out on the lake, running actual camps. Two different skill sets. Two different places to be. Contracts, permits, finances—that stuff's a full-time job and those were George's strengths. I belong out here." Her hand swung through the air. "In the trees, on the rocks, in the water, knee-deep in mud, interacting with the actual campers. Changing lives." She shrugged. "The camp's brain and the camp's heart are two different jobs. But what if George's investors don't understand the importance of the heart side?"

"Then you'll tell them and show them." Luke took her shoulders gently in his hands and turned her to face him. "The lodge was never Camp Spirit's heart. You are. It'll be your job to tell these new business drones how the day-to-day staff under you feel, what the campers really need, and make sure that they don't lose sight of what really matters." He cupped his fingers under her chin and tilted her face toward him. "I'm convinced, there is no one on earth who can do that better than you."

He lowered his mouth, intending to brush a gentle kiss across her cheek. Emergency vehicles peeled into the camp parking lot. Nicky jumped back. Her eyes darted to the flood of police. "I've got to go sort all this. When are you heading back to Toronto?"

"Soon, but not immediately. I'm going to call my editor, Vince, to see how he'd feel about my taking a couple of days off. I figure it'll take you a few cups of coffee, not to mention some long hikes through the woods, to get your head around where everything is at. It's been a rough couple of days and as a friend who's been through it all with you, I'd like to hang out here a bit, to help shoulder whatever bit of the load I can, just until things get back to normal."

A smile lit the golden flecks of her eyes. "I'd like that."

So would he. Luke watched as Nicky strode toward the police, her head held high, confident and in control. Then suddenly she turned, ran through the maze of vehicles and into the waiting arms of an old man stepping out of an unmarked police car—George.

Oh, Lord, guide their conversation. Help them heal together.

He walked to the closest officer, gave his name and pointed him in the direction of Trevor.

The day wore on. Luke hung by the edge of the emergency response people, giving answers when needed, staying out of the way when he wasn't. The sky was black. The camp was awash in a maze of red-and-blue emergency lights. Trevor was handcuffed and placed in the back of a police car. His father watched him go.

A sigh left Luke's chest. Finally it was done. The Hunter had been arrested. Authorities had dispatched

a boat to collect Russ and Bear's bodies from the island. Police statements had been given. Everyone was
home safe. The only thing left to do now was to make
sure Nicky was back on her feet, wrap up his time here
and eventually head back to Toronto with more dignity
and grace than he'd left here last time.

Luke's eyes ran down past the cabins to where she
now stood. Her body was a dark form against a back-
drop of the lodge's arched, fire-scarred wood. A blanket was wrapped around her shoulders. He'd caught
her, in that very spot, just a few days ago. He took a
deep breath and turned toward her. This time, he was
going to do things right.

"Luke?" George's face was pale in the flashing
lights. "Can we talk?"

A sad smile crossed Luke's face. He hesitated, then
hugged the older man tightly. George hugged him back
for a long moment before letting go. "I'm so sorry
about Trevor."

"Me, too. I wish…" George's words caught his
throat. "God is still good, you know? No matter what.
God can still get through to my son. I need to hold on
to that."

Luke nodded. "Me, too." Once again his eyes
dragged over to Nicky.

George gestured him toward a bench. They sat.

"Nicky tells me you're planning on bringing in a
handful of investors for this place," Luke said. "She's
worried about it, obviously. The idea of a new boss is
hard enough, let alone two or three. But I think it's a
really good idea."

"I'm glad." George followed Luke's gaze. "I know it's going to be hard for her. It's going to be a pretty big change. But, she's the best. The most talented outdoors instructor I've ever met. I couldn't imagine running this business without her as camp director—"

"You don't need to convince me." Luke grinned. "I know how spectacular Nicky is."

"Good. Because I'm too old to keep running all of this." A sigh rippled over George's shoulders. "We need fresh blood. We need people who can get us out of debt and then take the camp though the necessary steps to get charity status. Recently, I've really felt like God was nudging me that we need to do more for at-risk youth, too—runaways, those in trouble with the law, those who need a fresh start."

Luke nodded. "She told me. The island would be perfect for that."

"So, here's the plan," George said. "For the next few months I'm going to stay on full-time, retain the title of managing director and fifty-one percent ownership of the camp. The other codirectors will own forty-nine between them and commit to putting in a handful of hours a month."

Made sense. He could attract some serious professionals that way.

"Then, after the summer, I'm hoping to step down and hand my share of the camp over to a new managing director."

"Sounds solid."

George's eyes searched Luke's face. "I'd like that man to be you."

"Me?" Luke shot to his feet. "As managing director and majority owner of this place? You can't be serious!"

"Completely. I'd already discussed it with Trevor, and my lawyer has drawn up the paperwork." George stood slowly. "That's why I invited you up this weekend and why it mattered so much that Nicky got to know you. After Nicky, I can't think of anyone who understands the importance of what we're doing here more than you, and I needed to know if she saw in you the same things I did. She did and even more. Nicky told me how incredible you were. You were there for her. She said you were insightful, and strong, and took initiative, and she couldn't have made it through if it wasn't for you."

Maybe. But that hardly meant Nicky was prepared to accept Luke as the camp owner and her boss! She'd only just barely managed to forgive him for the past. There was no way he could ask Nicky to entrust her entire future to a man who'd let her down. "Are you sure about this, George? I have a seriously messed up past!"

"I know." The old man's eyes radiated the same hope and faith Luke had first seen in them years ago when George had stretched out his hand to help the runaway up off the floor. "But you also have a future, Luke. That's why the kids here need you. They need to see you, to hear you, to listen to you. They need your help to realize they have a future, too."

Luke nearly groaned. George made it all sound so simple. How could he do this to him? How could he sit there and offer him the chance to help Nicky build the camp of her dreams—their dreams—when Luke knew he was in no position to take it?

"George, do you even know what fifty-one percent of this place is worth? Even if I was the right man for this place, I'm in no position to buy even a sliver of your camp."

"I know." The older man's hand touched his shoulder. "Remember the camp cash box?"

Luke almost laughed. "How could I forget? I stole it. You reminded me of it when I pulled you out of the fire on Thursday."

George nodded. "Because I didn't know if I'd survive and I knew my will would come out. We had this exact same argument, years ago in the police station, when I stood there and emptied out the contents of the camp cash box to cover your bail."

"Because I didn't deserve your kindness or your money."

"I know. But it's not about deserving or being able to pay for it, Luke. I've decided to give my camp to you."

Dark water lapped the shore by her feet. She felt Luke behind her and knew it was him without even turning. She'd always known when it was him, even as she'd waited for him on the lookout years ago as a teenager. She'd known his approach from the sound of his footfall on the ground and the subtle sound his throat made just before he opened his mouth to speak. She'd known it from the way every inch of every muscle inside her body ached to turn around and run into his arms.

"Nicky, I'm sorry. Things have changed. I've got to go."

She didn't even look at him. Hot tears rushed to her eyes and spilled down her cheeks before she could even think to stop them. Of course. Luke was leaving again. Just when she'd begun to let her guard down and trust him, just when he'd promised her he'd be hanging around for a while, he was running away. Again. She didn't even turn. "Well, thanks for everything. Safe travels."

"Believe me. I'm so sorry to do this. Really. But George just dropped something pretty heavy duty on my lap. Asked me something pretty major, I can't possibly say yes to. He's told me he wants me to take some time to think and pray before I give him an answer. I promised I would, even though the answer's going to be no." He sighed. "I just need to be alone right now. I need to not be here."

A bitter laugh rose to the edge of her teeth. "So, you finally found out what reason George had for inviting you up here, and your immediate reaction was to turn him down and leave."

"Please. Look at me." The warmth of his fingertips brushed against her neck. "It's not that simple."

"I shouldn't even be surprised. George should've known this is what would happen." She blinked hard and wiped the tears from her eyes. "If you're going to go, just go. Don't put me through this again."

"Nicky!" His voice rose as her name left his lips. "That's not fair. It's not like I wanted to disappoint

George. I have to. And do you really think for one moment that I *want* to leave you?"

She turned. There he was, inches away from her, his eyes filled with a passion and longing that took her breath away. But his shoulders slumped like a man who'd decided he was defeated, without even waiting for the first blow.

"Don't you get how I feel about you?" His hand slid along the side of her face. His fingers brushed though her hair. "I admire you. You're strong, inside and out. You're compassionate. You love other people. You even loved a wretch like me when no one else would." He groaned, like a drowning man, watching his only chance at rescue drifting away. "I would give anything to help your dreams come true. I just can't."

"I like you, too, Luke." No, she loved him. Still loved him. Deeply. Completely. She'd always loved him. She probably always would. "But I'm not going to just stand here and listen to you give up on yourself." Tears spilled from her eyes now. She didn't even bother wiping them away. It was about time she let him see what he'd put her through.

"I'm tired of watching you act like you've got nothing to offer anyone, and tired of standing back and watching you listen to the lies in your head. You think I haven't seen this expression on your face before? I don't know what George said to you or what he asked you to do. I don't care at this point." Her voice broke. "All I know is I'm tired trying to convince you to believe in yourself."

She brushed her hands along his cheeks and felt the

bristles of his jaw underneath her fingertips. "You told Gracie that God would give her a new life. All she had to do was reach out and take it. You are the strongest, bravest, most incredible man I know. You can do anything. You can be anything. You faced down a killer. You saved my life." Her voice whispered over his skin. "You can handle anything."

His head shook. "Not this." His lips brushed over her tears. "Not what George has asked of me. Not knowing every time I look in your eyes that there's nothing I want more than to be here, stay here with you, forever, yet feeling with every breath that fills my chest that I'm not the man that you need."

She closed her eyes. "Then you're right. You're not the man I need around. Goodbye Luke. Take care of yourself."

She kissed his cheek then pushed him back gently. He left without looking back.

TWENTY

September's morning light danced along the surface of the lake. Nicky zipped the soft red sweatshirt all the way to the top, then pulled her hood over her hair. Tips of orange and yellow had already begun to peek through the forest of green. The leaves were turning early this year.

Camp Spirit had survived another summer. Her eyes drifted to the heavens. *Thank You, Lord.* With some neighborly help from Ace Sports, lodge activities had moved into a portable event tent for the summer. The generous donation of a cooking trailer from a local food truck chain had served as their mobile kitchen. She chuckled. It had taken a whole bunch of wrangling, not to mention a lot of flexibility, but they'd made it. It would definitely be a summer the campers would never forget.

The national press had been all over the camp in the days following Trevor's arrest, stirring up more support and generosity than she'd have ever imagined. *Torchlight News* has sent a fun and tenacious female reporter to cover the story. She hadn't heard a word from Luke since he'd walked out of her life the night the Hunter was finally caught. But while thoughts of him drifted through her heart daily, there was a peace there, too. She'd let him go this time. She'd respected herself. There was peace in that.

Trevor had pled guilty, saving his already emotionally battered father the stress of a long, drawn-out trial. Last she'd heard, Trevor was still refusing to talk to George, no matter how many times his father had driven to Sudbury to visit him. She sighed as she prayed. *Lord, have mercy.*

The clatter of hammers and saws echoed through the trees behind her. The loss of Bear had hit both his company and the community pretty hard. Bear and Russ had had funerals days after the police had recovered their bodies from the island, and the Ontario community would never be the same.

But over the following weeks and months, George's plan to find new codirectors for the camp had slowly taken shape. One of the first had been Sunny Shield, CEO of Shields Construction—a beautiful, raven-haired woman with a growing interest in both community involvement and faith.

Thanks to Shields Construction the new lodge and kitchens would be up before the first snow fell. It was pretty clear from what George had said, the new codirectors first order of business was to fix the financial situation and apply for charitable status. But becoming an official charity was easier said than done. The process was a lot of work and would take clearing some major debts and getting the camp on a more secure footing. All the more reason to bring on codirectors to help them through the process.

She hadn't met all the new board yet and still wasn't sure whether the camp's new direction made her more excited or nervous. After several long discussions with George, they'd decided she would focus all her energy on directing the camp smoothly through another summer season, while he managed the ins and outs of interviewing potential codirectors and evaluating options. It wasn't exactly easy to let go of her fears. But she trusted him. More than that, she trusted God, herself and that no matter what happened next God would help her through it.

Now it was time to put that trust into action. Yesterday, the new codirectors had held their first major meeting—confirming they were all in and shared the same vision. Papers had been signed. The deal was done. Which meant today was the day George was going to introduce her to them, in preparation for making the big announcement to the press.

She heard footsteps coming down the path behind her. *Well, Lord, here we go.* A smile lit her face. It was Tabitha. The politician somehow managed to look as crisp and professional as ever even in jeans and a windbreaker. They hugged. "Please tell me this means you've decided to invest in our ragtag little camp?"

The grandmother-to-be smiled. "Absolutely. I've decided not to run for reelection and this seemed the perfect new venture to get involved in."

"How's Gracie?"

Tabitha's smile softened. "She's well. It's been a bit challenging, but thankfully the university let her defer for a year and she's managing to keep most of her scholarship money. She still hasn't heard a word from David. He was pretty angry that she decided to keep the baby and made it clear he wanted nothing to do with them. But his brother Aaron's been at every doctor's appointment. As they say, it's a bit complicated."

Nicky nodded. She could imagine.

"Now, this is more than just a social visit." Tabitha's tone grew serious. "As you know, the new board met yesterday, and I'm here on their behalf with an offer. Two offers, in fact."

Nicky's heart rate sped up a notch. "What kinds of offers?"

"Can we sit?"

Nicky nodded. They crossed to a picnic table. *Lord, I didn't prepare for this...*

Tabitha pulled a manila envelope from inside her jacket and set it on the table between them. "It was very important in our meeting yesterday that we considered how this new arrangement would impact on you. We discussed it at length, in fact. You are obviously an extremely important part of this camp, and with George stepping down, yours would become the primary face of this camp in the community. One of the new co-owners felt strongly it was important you had a way out in case this new situation didn't sit right with you. To that end, we're prepared to offer you a year's salary as severance, a glowing recommendation and the services of a professional headhunter. It was felt quite strongly many camps across the country would jump at the chance to have you."

In fact, Ace Sports had already offered her a very generous salary package, but she hadn't actually wanted to leave. *Lord, I keep asking what Your will is and I have to listen to what You're telling me. Is Your answer in this envelope?*

"Does this mean the new co-owners would like me to leave?"

Tabitha laughed. She reached across the table and took both Nicky's hands in hers. "No, honey. Not at all. It means no one wants you to feel trapped here if you'd rather go." She sat back and pulled out a second envelope. "In fact, we're very much hoping the second offer is more to your liking. The new managing director has suggested we give you a small percent of the camp. That would make you both a codirector and co-owner of this camp. It would give you a vote and a say at the table, but no obligation to sit through any boring meetings or discussions you don't want to. Our new managing director felt quite strongly in fact that we needed to hear from you and that you needed to have a voice as an advocate for the staff and campers."

The woman's words tickled at the back of her memory. A tiny flicker of hope brushed the edges of her heart. She'd heard someone stand by this water's edge and say those very words before. But, could it be…?

Nicky stood. "Thank you. These are two very generous offers and I'm more grateful than I can say. Yes, it might be hard to get my head around new co-owners and a new vision, but I love this camp and believe in it with my whole heart. So as long as you're willing to stick through it with me, I'm willing to stick through it with you."

"Wonderful." Tabitha stood and shook Nicky's hand. Then she glanced over Nicky's shoulder. "He told me you'd probably say that."

"Who?" Nicky turned.

But no sooner had the words left her lips, than she saw the tall, broad-shouldered man in blue jeans, a blazer and tie leaning against a tree. Her heart rose in her chest.

Luke started down the path toward her. Tabitha said something to him quietly, then smiled and walked back up toward to the construction site.

Nicky barely noticed her go. Her eyes swept over Luke. The lines of his shoulders were stronger and more confident than when she'd seen him last. But his eyes—oh, his eyes—their depths shone with the same intensity that had haunted her dreams for years.

"Hi, Nicky."

"Hi." She crossed her arms in front of her chest. She could feel a smile curling up at the edges of her lips. "So, let me get this straight. I don't hear from you for months. No letters, no emails, not so much as a phone call. Then you show up here, unannounced, and try to convince me to leave this place?"

"No. I came back here feeling foolish for the doubts that drove me away, thankful that you gave me the kick I needed to work through them, and hoping very, very much you'd be willing to stay."

Understanding filled her heart. "So that thing

George asked of you that you didn't feel capable of...
was to take over as the new managing director."

He nodded. "I'm sorry, Nicky. In that moment the
doubts were clanging so loudly in my mind, I had
to run away from here to see that this is where I belonged." He stepped toward her, so close now she could
almost feel the gentle rise and fall of his breath in his
chest brush against her still-folded arms.

"The funny thing is, it took me hours. Mere hours
to know you were right, that I could let go of the past
and be the kind of man this camp needed at its helm.
That I could be the kind of man you needed me to be.
But by that point, what could I do? I couldn't pursue
a relationship with you knowing I might become your
boss. It was a double-edged sword. The one thing pulling me toward you seemed to be the very thing forcing us apart."

She nodded. "I understand."

His fingers brushed along her arms, gently prying
them apart. "Trust me, waiting for this day to come,
waiting to be here talking to you, has been the most
agonizing wait of my life."

She let him pull her arms apart, tingling with the
brush of his fingers on her skin. "Do you honestly think
I want you to be my boss?"

"No." A smile crossed his lips, setting warmth alight
in his eyes. "But I'm hoping you're willing to be my
partner, Nicky, in this camp and in my life. Which is
why I fought tooth and nail for you to get a percent-
age of this camp. Taking it out of my share, in fact.
Giving you just enough that if I lose my edge, and if

you ever side against me with the other directors, I'm forced into a stalemate." His fingers brushed along her palms. "See, there's no way I could ever hope to run this place without you. I need you, Nicky. This camp needs you—this complicated, scrappy, determined, beautiful place that is so very, terribly, inexorably you."

His hands slid around her waist. Her hands slid around his neck. He pulled her closer still until she could feel his heart beating into hers.

"Nicky, please…" His voice brushed gruffly against her ear. "Please, tell me, officially, you're either taking the severance package or agreeing to become a co-owner and codirector. Because until you do, I'm still your pending boss, so I can't let myself kiss you…and I've been waiting to kiss you for so very long."

Her eyes closed. His lips nibbled her neck, sending shivers dancing down her skin. She ran her fingers through his wild, dark hair. "Promise me you'll never run away again."

He pulled back, just enough that he could look into her eyes. "Nicky Trailer, my friend, my beauty, who has shared her heart, mind and strength with me—I admire you, I respect you, I need you and, above all, I love you. You have held my heart in your hands ever since we first met in these woods so many years ago, and I am done running away from being a man worthy of you." He curled her hair between his fingers. "I'm not going anywhere. I am in love with you, Nicky, and I always will be."

Joy danced in her eyes like sunlight on the water.

"I love you, too, Luke. And yes, together, we're going to make this place something great."

He glanced to the sky above. *"Thank You, God!"*

A cool breeze shook the trees around them and leaves cascaded down, as gently but firmly his mouth found hers in a kiss.

* * * * *

Dear Reader,

Right now, I'm sitting in a wood cabin on the shores of Lake Rousseau, Ontario, watching trees dance in the breeze. It's been a year since an enthusiastic young man—one of two great twins who work here—helped me brainstorm ways these woods, lake and people might inspire a story.

What I love about Luke and Nicky is that they're both struggling to overcome things in their pasts. Both, in different ways, are afraid of change. Last year, I doubted whether I'd ever be able to translate all the fledgling ideas I got from these woods into the book you're now holding in your hands. In the same way, sometimes it's hard to believe what's happened in our past won't always shape our future.

Like the twins who encouraged me, I pray you'll find people in your lives who'll help you through challenges, adventures and struggles you face.

Thank you so much for sharing this journey with me. To find out more about me and about my books, please visit me online at www.maggiekblack.com and follow me on Twitter at @maggiekblack.

Every blessing,

Maggie

COMING NEXT MONTH FROM
Love Inspired® Suspense

Available March 3, 2015

PROTECTION DETAIL
Capitol K-9 Unit • by Shirlee McCoy
A congressman is shot, and Capitol K-9 Unit captain
Gavin McCord promises to protect all in the marksman's path.
When a foster mother and children are added to the target list,
Gavin must bring the culprit to justice before he strikes again.

STRANDED
Military Investigations • by Debby Giusti
Colleen Brennan is trying to bring down a drug trafficking
scheme. But when a wild twister traps her in an Amish town,
she must rely on Special Agent Frank Gallagher to get out alive.

HIDDEN AGENDA • by Christy Barritt
To find his father's murderer, CIA operative Ed Carter enlists
the help of nurse Bailey Williams. But now they're both in the
sight line of a cold-blooded killer...

UNTRACEABLE
Mountain Cove • by Elizabeth Goddard
As search and rescue volunteers, Isaiah Callahan and
Heidi Warren never anticipated being lured into a trap set by
robbers. Now they'll need to outwit their captors—if they
can forge through deadly icy terrain first.

BROKEN SILENCE • by Annslee Urban
When someone wants Amber Talbot dead, her ex-fiancé—and
detective on the case—must keep her safe. Patrick Wiley
agrees to put their history aside...to help the woman he hasn't
been able to forget.

DANGEROUS INHERITANCE • by Barbara Warren
Macy Douglas returns to her childhood home searching for
answers. When an unknown attacker determines to keep
Macy from digging up her family's past, officer Nick Baldwin
must uncover the ruthless criminal's identity before they're
sent six feet under.

LOOK FOR THESE AND OTHER LOVE INSPIRED BOOKS WHEREVER
BOOKS ARE SOLD, INCLUDING MOST BOOKSTORES, SUPERMARKETS,
DISCOUNT STORES AND DRUGSTORES.

LISCNM0215

REQUEST YOUR FREE BOOKS!

2 FREE RIVETING INSPIRATIONAL NOVELS
PLUS 2 FREE MYSTERY GIFTS

YES! Please send me 2 FREE Love Inspired® Suspense novels and my 2 FREE mystery gifts (gifts are worth about $10). After receiving them, if I don't wish to receive any more books, I can return the shipping statement marked "cancel." If I don't cancel, I will receive 4 brand-new novels every month and be billed just $4.74 per book in the U.S. or $5.24 per book in Canada. That's a savings of at least 21% off the cover price. It's quite a bargain! Shipping and handling is just 50¢ per book in the U.S. and 75¢ per book in Canada.* I understand that accepting the 2 free books and gifts places me under no obligation to buy anything. I can always return a shipment and cancel at any time. Even if I never buy another book, the two free books and gifts are mine to keep forever.

123/323 IDN F5AC

Name _____ (PLEASE PRINT) _____

Address _____ Apt. #

City _____ State/Prov. _____ Zip/Postal Code

Signature (if under 18, a parent or guardian must sign)

Mail to the Harlequin® Reader Service:
IN U.S.A.: P.O. Box 1867, Buffalo, NY 14240-1867
IN CANADA: P.O. Box 609, Fort Erie, Ontario L2A 5X3

**Are you a current subscriber to Love Inspired Suspense books
and want to receive the larger-print edition?
Call 1-800-873-8635 or visit www.ReaderService.com.**

* Terms and prices subject to change without notice. Prices do not include applicable taxes. Sales tax applicable in N.Y. Canadian residents will be charged applicable taxes. Offer not valid in Quebec. This offer is limited to one order per household. Not valid for current subscribers to Love Inspired Suspense books. All orders subject to credit approval. Credit or debit balances in a customer's account(s) may be offset by any other outstanding balance owed by or to the customer. Please allow 4 to 6 weeks for delivery. Offer available while quantities last.

Your Privacy—The Harlequin® Reader Service is committed to protecting your privacy. Our Privacy Policy is available online at www.ReaderService.com or upon request from the Harlequin Reader Service.
We make a portion of our mailing list available to reputable third parties that offer products we believe may interest you. If you prefer that we not exchange your name with third parties, or if you wish to clarify or modify your communication preferences, please visit us at www.ReaderService.com/consumerschoice or write to us at Harlequin Reader Service Preference Service, P.O. Box 9062, Buffalo, NY 14269. Include your complete name and address.

LIS13R

SPECIAL EXCERPT FROM

Love Inspired.
SUSPENSE

*Murder and mayhem are plaguing the nation's capital,
and it's up to the Capitol K-9 Unit to restore order.*

*Read on for a sneak preview of PROTECTION DETAIL
by Shirlee McCoy, the first book in the exciting new
CAPITOL K-9 UNIT series.*

Michael Jeffries was dead, and there wasn't one thing
Capitol K-9 Unit Captain Gavin McCord could do about
it. It seemed inconceivable, impossible, but it was true.
Michael had been a good guy, a great attorney. Fair-
minded, reasonable and determined to always see justice
done. Now he was gone, shot down in the prime of his
life.

That hurt. A lot.

Gavin snapped a picture of the bloodstain on the pave-
ment at the rear of congressman Harland Jefferies's man-
sion. He'd already had the evidence team collect samples
for DNA. He knew they'd find DNA matching Michael Jeffries and his father. Like Michael, Harland had been shot by
a small-caliber handgun.

Unlike his father, the young lawyer hadn't survived.

Sad. All the way around.

Gavin knew and liked both of the men, but he couldn't
let his emotions get in the way of the investigation. He
snapped another picture, glanced around the scene. The DC
police had been the first responders, and several officers
were huddled together discussing the case. He knew most

of them. He'd worked as a DC police officer for ten years before taking the job Margaret Meyer had offered him. It had been an opportunity he couldn't pass up, one that he hadn't *wanted* to pass up.

Glory shifted beside him. The three-year-old shepherd was too well-trained to stand before she was told to, but it was obvious that the excitement of the crime scene was making her antsy.

"Be patient," he said.

"McCord!" one of the DC officers waved him over.

"What's up?" he asked, approaching Dane, his gaze jumping to the bloodstained concrete where Harland had been lying. Michael's body had been found a few feet away.

"One of my men found something near the tree line. I thought you might want to see it." Dane held up an evidence bag with a bright blue mitten in it. "Thing was clean as a whistle. Not a leaf on it. Not a stick. Not a speck of grass covering it."

"It looks like a kid's mitten," he said. They had a possible witness!

Don't miss
PROTECTION DETAIL by Shirlee McCoy,
available March 2015 wherever
Love Inspired® Suspense books are sold.

LISEXP0215

Annie stood by the dessert table when she saw Jedidiah Lapp chatting with his wife, Sarah. She'd been heartbroken when Jed had broken up with her, and then married Sarah Mast.

Seeing the two of them together was a reminder of what she didn't have. Annie wanted a husband—and a family. But how could she marry when no one showed an interest in her? She blinked back tears. She'd work hard to be a wife a husband would appreciate. She wanted children, to hold a baby in her arms, a child to nurture and love.

She sniffled, looked down and straightened the dessert table. And the pitchers and jugs of iced tea and lemonade.

"May I have some lemonade?" a deep, familiar voice said.

Annie looked up. "Jacob." His expression was serious as he studied her. She glanced down and noticed the fine dusting of corn residue on his dark jacket. "Lemonade?" she echoed self-consciously.

"*Ja*. Lemonade," he said with amusement.

She quickly reached for the pitcher. She poured his lemonade into a plastic cup, only chancing a glance at him when she handed him his drink.

"How is the work going?" she asked conversationally.

"We are nearly finished with the corn. We'll be cutting hay next." He lifted the glass to his lips and took a swallow.

Warmth pooled in her stomach as she watched the movement of his throat. "How's *Dat?*" she asked. She had seen him chatting with her father earlier.

Jacob glanced toward her *dat* with a small smile. "He says he's not tired. He claims he's enjoying the view too much." His smile dissipated. "No doubt he'll be exhausted later."

Annie agreed. "I'll check on him in a while." She hesitated. "Are you hungry? I can fix you a plate—"

He gazed at her for several heartbeats with his striking golden eyes. "*Ne,* I'll fix one myself." He finished his drink and held out his glass to her. "May I?"

She hurried to refill his glass. With a crooked smile and a nod of thanks, Jacob accepted the refill and left. The warm flutter in her stomach grew stronger as she watched him walk away, stopping briefly to chat with Noah and Rachel, his brother and sister-in-law.

Annie glanced over where several men were being dished up plates of food. She then caught sight of Jacob walking along with his brother Eli. The contrast of Jacob's dark hair and Eli's light locks struck her as they disappeared into the barn. They came out a few minutes later, Eli carrying tools, Jacob leading one of her father's workhorses.

As if he sensed her regard, Jacob looked over and locked gazes with her.

Will Annie ever find the husband of her heart?
Pick up A WIFE FOR JACOB to find out.
Available March 2015,
wherever Love Inspired® books and ebooks are sold.